Dark March

Stories for When the
Rest of the World is Asleep

Colin Fleming

Outpost19 | San Francisco
outpost19.com

Fleming, Colin
        Dark March: Stories for When the Rest of the World
        is Asleep / Colin Fleming
        ISBN 9781937402563 (pbk)
        ISBN 9781937402570 (ebook)

Cover art and design by Jenny Gorecki

Library of Congress Control Number: 2013907892

OUTPOST
19

PROVOCATIVE READING
SAN FRANCISCO
NEW YORK
OUTPOST19.COM

For John Musok, who understood and cared—and listened—more than anyone else. With all my love, gratitude, and thankfulness that you will never have to know what I have known. The next malt beer (blah) is on me, be it in this world or the next. (And yes, yours can be a 40 ouncer. As if it could have been otherwise.)

The Spit

It was the gull who first noticed that the island had left. Not that he was the only gull, although he thought of himself that way. But the island was definitely not there, one morning, when the gull arrived with his breakfast crab. He liked to dine on the island, because the island also made for a good plate, and table too, come to think of it. Some crabs were tougher than others, naturally, and when the gull found that his beak would not do, he'd drop his breakfast crab out of the air, and it'd open up nicely on the island, and he could eat in peace.

But the island was definitely not there on that particular morning. There was no arguing that. The gull, besides, had an excellent sense of direction, and he had been dining at the island for years. It was a standby for him. He had tried not to get caught up in the debates, as many others had. Well, as some others had. It had been argued, for centuries, whether the island was a proper island, or part of the coast, like the boulder that was twenty yards to the north, and closer to the edge, for that is what islands—official or otherwise—called the land that none of them ever got to visit. He was close to the edge as well; would a real island be thusly situated? There was talk of him being an oxymoron, if he were, indeed, to remain an island. The geologists would quarrel, while the cartographers, having less and less respect for the quarreling geologists, would get up to their varieties of mischief-making, which was not so exciting as everyone else—the gull and the other gulls, included—knew.

They would call the island an island, when it suited them, or a mound of rocks, when it did not. Maps could be frightfully limiting, in terms of how much space one had to work with; sometimes, the more details a cartographer wanted to put in—some liked to include asides on the currents, the contours of the bottom of that portion of the coast, or even figures representing the shapes of the headlands—the easier it was to call the island nothing at all, because it saved a few letters. And besides—no one had ever really gotten it right, in that you could call the pile of rocks, where the gull took his breakfast, whatever you pleased, and have your supporters. Naturally, your supporters would be spread across centuries, because whom, really, would you come across in your daily life to discuss this matter with? And this provided the island with an opportunity.

He had been a jumble or rocks for as long as he could remember. He didn't have any trees, or bushes, unless one counted the beard of barnacles that covered his outer edges. There was a high school football field off in the distance, where the Lobster Men played. These were different Lobster Men, of course, from the lobster men who skirted around his edges, returning to the land, where the trees and bushes stood. Some of those trees and bushes would wave to him, or in his general direction, anyway, when the wind decided to come out and play, but he wasn't sure if that made them friends, or just acquaintances.

In earlier times, after he'd been there a few thousand centuries, the lobster men would trip over him in their boats, and on several occasions their bodies became tangled beneath him. Or it felt like that, anyway. There really wasn't a "beneath him" him in the regular sense, where other things moved around. He went down to the bottom, but, then again, he was only two or three football fields from where the trees and plants were, if he could trust the measuring devices of the Lobster Men (for that is what he assumed football fields were) who'd never, so far as he knew, become tangled in him, although there was a chance they could grow up and end up in such a state.

One time in particular was especially horrible. The head was like one of the eggs, only bigger, that a local heron—who at least understood, unlike the gull, that there were other herons (they even had a system of nomenclature, so that they might distinguish between themselves)—had tried to leave on him, despite his efforts to suggest that one of the places with trees and bushes would probably work better, for he was more of a loner, and it did not seem like the heron and he were suitable companions, even for a short period of time.

He hung out with the waves, naturally, but everyone, just about, did that in his circle. You couldn't shake those waves. And what inconstant fellows; a wave would come by one time, and it was always just the one time, like he had better things to do, on the other side of him, closer to where the trees and plants were. He'd watch the waves get out of the water. That was impressive. Got straight out, and headed up the beach. And then into the beach. It never failed to amaze him that waves could be so ambulatory, and go wherever they pleased. Ah, that was the stuff! The pleasure, the privilege, of coming and going as you liked. True, the waves could be brutal, and maybe it was that brutality that empowered them.

No one would ever let it be said—not the crabs who hurtled through the air, the gull with his singular belief in his uniqueness, the herons with their nomenclature, or the beard of barnacles—that the waves did not inspire respect, regardless of their penchant—when afforded the opportunity—for brutality. Like with that lobster man's head, which became softer each day in the water, and more and more egg-like, as the battering army of waves drove it, again and again, against him, against his will, until finally it broke and caved in against the island's toughest portion, the corner of himself that he had previously been most proud of, where his granite was like felsic razors, capable of fighting off any other island, if it came to that, although it had been years since any of the islands had battled the others.

Most days passed the same as all the days before. The plants and shrubs would wave, and the island would lament his lot as an island who could not make like the waves. That is, until he learned that he was to be an island no more, nor a pile of rocks. A man came to him. He measured him, he felt his beard of barnacles, he probed his underside. He discovered a part of the island the island himself was unaware of. He had a leg. Sure, it was not a standard leg. Most islands with standard legs showed them off, so that everyone else could see; that is, they were above water, and those legs made them not islands, but rather spits. And that is what Herbert Schrimschmidt determined him to be.

"Yes, that is what you are," he declared, after a final day of study. "Connected to the land by a granite ledge that originates near the center of this...island. Pile of rocks." The island, who was about to officially become a spit, wanted to thank the great man, for he assumed he could be no less than that. All of these years, and the mystery that he himself had no solution for, was at last solved. Was this exciting? Was this the point of all of the thousands of centuries? Is this what the glacier meant when she said, "Go forth, my son, and score this earth, as best you can, and leave your mark, as here I have left you."

That was some impassioned speech. Still, he had his doubts that she hadn't made it to all of his brothers and sisters, along the way. She was well-traveled, to put it politely. The waves would not have been so delicate.

"Fucking whore's bastard" one shouted as it careened past him, like a missile, during one of the almighty storms, when the waves were launched from the sea, and he remained where he always remained, grateful, for once, to be so securely anchored. He was a fixed point, and knew it. But usually, that was a downer, because his opportunities for adventure were limited.

The birds would boast endlessly about theirs. He couldn't do anything but listen. Where was he going to go? One of the gulls would tell tall tales about the affairs he had had "out of species," meaning, so the island thought, affairs that did not center on working himself over, as some of the amoebas did.

"So I'm nailing this chickadee, right, and this bitch is like, 'Oh, Mr. Gull, damn, Mr. Gull," and I'm like, "Call me Gully, bitch, say my name," and she's like, "Gully, Gully, Gully!' You hear me island? Hot, right? Got me a date with a crow tonight. Little white on black, if you know what I mean. And then a different kind of white on black, if you know what I double mean. High five!" At this point, the gull would peck the island with his beak. The island was grateful when bottles with trace levels of alcohol would wash up on him, especially if the gull had recently visited. They helped take the edge off, and made it easier to forget the gull's boastings.

"Time to make it official," Herbert Schrimschmidt stated, patting the island who was about to become, officially, a spit, on top of his tallest rock. "Now don't you go anywhere in the meanwhile."

"What a thing to say," the island, who was starting to consider himself as a spit, thought as Herbert paddled his dingy back to the edge.

"I'll say," added the rock crab who sometimes dined on his south side, where the less intelligent minnows hung out, and got themselves caught in the tidal currents.

Now, this was not a crab to be trusted. True, he was at times ingenious. He'd be hauled up on the boats, with the lobsters, and every single time, he'd get tossed back into the water. No one knew how he did it; the rock crab said it was a matter of his way with words, and his incomparable wit. As he was known for saying: Logic was enviable, but wit was influential.

But he was also a dick. When the urchins all started dying because of some dye that had gotten into the water, he went around gathering them up in this bucket he had found, selling their spindles—which were most effective as weapons, and for fence-building, which was, at that time, all the rage, with the local real estate boom, so that you could maintain your privacy—at cut-rate prices or in exchange for minnows. He was a glutton for minnows. The spit—nee, island—knew to be wary of the rock crab, but still, he was worth listening to, so long as you did so judiciously.

"Now's your chance, you know. If you wanted to go to the edge. I've been to the edge loads."

This, at least, was true. The spit had seen the rock crab up on the edge, not very far from the trees and plants, walking in the sand, nibbling on the trash he found there. The rock crab had extreme tastes. Still, he did not get along with the gull who did the boasting, and that gave him some credit, at least, in the eyes of the spit, which he figured were the spaces between his fifteen or so rocks. He had many eyes, like a scallop, even, but his were bigger, and this made him proud. The rock crab knew pride when he saw it, even if it was a temporary pride.

"My chance for what?"

"You're off the books right now, boyo. You're not anything."

"I'm a spit. Herbert said so."

"Yeah, of course he did. I heard him. Relax. But he's got to file everything. Your old status is in flux right now. So you don't have to stay here. There's nothing keeping you. You're off the grid, baby."

"The grid?"

"The water. If you want to be. Geez, you're naïve. What are you, like seven?"

"I'm like seven million."

"It's just a joke, son. Keep it together."

The rock crab sure had a splashy way of talking. The waves might like how he put that. Maybe he'd try out his new joke—although he didn't like to gossip—one of these days. But now was the time for listening.

"So you're footloose and fancy free. Think of it like being alive before you were born."

This was very heady.

"Go on."

"Well, if you knew you were about to be born, but you weren't yet, you're not anything, right? What could you do then? Any fucking thing you pleased. Until you were born. Then you'd be the thing you were. And you'd have to accept that. What an opportunity. I'd almost say I envied you, if I wasn't so…"

"Yes, I know. Ambulatory."

"That's right, baby. But why don't you make the most of your chance? Why don't you, you know…"

"No? Really?"

"Yeah. Go the edge. Have a spree. How long have you been here?"

"Like I said, seven million years."

"So you really deserve it then. Do your thing. Only do it soon. Now I gotta roll. Some of those dumbass jellyfish keep getting themselves trapped by the jetty"—the spit and the jetty were distant cousins, and they both liked getting news about the other—"so I'm going to drink a bunch of them down. You don't know what mesoglea is until you've drank jellyfish mesoglea. Mega delicious."

"Okay, rock crab. Thanks."

"No problem…what do you want me to call you?"

"Call me the spit," came the firm, proud reply.

"You got it, spit. Happy travels."

Come the evening, with the sound of the last of the fog horns still in his ears, which were, intriguingly enough, the same as his eyes, he was off. The gull who enjoyed his breakfast upon him each morning heard his crab drop into the water, with the triumphant report of "yahooooo!"

"I don't normally miss," he thought. "I'll try again."

And so he did, and missed again. And it was then he realized—

"Good fuck. He's gone. How can that be? I wouldn't be surprised if that braggart of a fellow…so strange he is, can't even tell what species he belongs to…had something to do with this. I saw him with a cardinal the other day. And you know what they say about cardinals. You can trust a cardinal about as well as you can trust a…"

But he understood he was getting off subject. He'd have to go hungry, that morning. Besides: he wasn't in the mood to eat. Something was very wrong, he felt.

And indeed it was. For no one had requested to look at the maps that detailed the specifics of the water, and the edge, for a long, long time, and the main map that was held in the basement of the building that Herbert Schrimschmidt finally got himself to (his discovery had necessitated a celebratory spree of his own, which he undertook in the next town over, as that town was more hardscrabble than the one where the spit, the rock crab, and the two gulls lived, and where you could drink the day away in the company of out-of-work fisherman, with whom Herbert liked to think he had something in common) fell to pieces when he began to work upon it. A replacement would have to be made, but that would take time.

In the meanwhile, everyone became ambulatory, more ambulatory, than ever. The water switched sides with the edge, the moon went to the side of the sky where the sun liked to be, and the sun went to where you'd normally find the moon. So it turned out that no one missed the spit at all, since it looked, more or less, like he was where he always was, especially once the world turned over, and what had been up was now down. He wasn't, of course, where he had always been, but as the rock crab pointed out to a hermit crab who had made a disgusting face while the former drank down some jellyfish remains: "Perception is a fickle bitch. Fancy some jellyfish mesoglea?"

The hermit crab, who was a most educated hermit crab—he'd read every last word of every random page of every book or magazine that he chanced upon—wouldn't even deign to disabuse the rock crab of the notion that there was such a thing as jellyfish. They weren't fish. They were, more technically speaking, jellies. But he was not above a tart literary reference that would be lost upon the rock crab.

"Enjoy your Slough of Despond, my chap, enjoy your Slough of Despond."

"Right on, brother. Right on. You too."

Eventually, Herbert began to put map matters right, and everyone started to realize that if they all got caught in flux—*in flagrante delicto*, as the literary hermit crab put it—why, they were going to blow a good thing. The gull who had just propositioned and been turned down by a ring-necked pheasant was listening in on this meeting—which was held, as these meetings always are, from across vast distances—and made a crude joke, but the others paid him no mind. He was that kind of gull. Thankfully, they'd all been reading the papers. Well, you couldn't help but read the papers. They were bound to blow your way, at some time or other. There was this Super Bowl thing, and they could move about in safety, that night. The streets would be deserted, it seemed.

So it came that the sun sheepishly passed the moon, who was equally sheepish, and the edge went back to where it had been, nodding to the water as it did so. The gull who thought he was the only gull in the world, who had become the most forlorn of gulls, thanks to the absence of his treasured breakfast routine, dropped his latest crab out of the sky, anticipating the now familiar plink of crustacean hitting water. He didn't know why he bothered anymore. Tradition, perhaps. Or the sort of homage that doubled as a lament. The hermit crab had been lecturing him on what he knew about requiems, which was, in sum, that they weren't supposed to be danced to. Best as he could tell. But this time, there was the solid, resonant response of crab bouncing off granite.

"What the fuck!" the rock crab screamed out, as the hard surface of the spit, however unwittingly, robbed him of his left claw. He rolled down into one of the many eyes/ears, before the gull who thought he was the only gull could claim his breakfast treat, but at least he knew that he'd probably be able to start the next day right. The wind blew the detached claw down into the socket/canal where the rock crab was presently tasting his own blood as it floated in the water.

"Fat load of good it will do me now," he bemoaned. "What are you doing here anyway? I thought we talked about you having a spree, and me getting in some well-deserved recreation as an aerialist?"

"I don't recall that part," the spit countered. "Are you sure?"

"Why else would I partner with that moron of a gull?"

This was a fair point. But the rock crab wondered if

maybe he'd been mistaken, given that the spit seemed to possess a surety of purpose that he had not had before. He'd have to be crafty.

"So what did you learn? Come on. Dish."

Silence.

"Well? Speak up, unless you're too scared. Are you too scared, spit?"

The truth was, the rock crab, despite his reputation, wasn't nearly as ambulatory as he liked everyone to believe. He was curious, to say the least, about the world beyond the edge.

"Come on, man, I'm bleeding out here. What am I going to do if I end up with a chance to roam around again, all footloose and fancy free, before I am something again, if it works that way. Is the edge worth my time?"

"A guy like you would do alright for himself on the edge. Very well indeed."

"Well. That's good to know, anyway," the rock crab concluded, as he bled out, and the gull who thought he was the only gull returned, upon second thought, to try to retrieve the rock crab's corpse—for a meal, for a homage that one could dance to, nobody knew.

"I've been talking to this guy who I think is a parrot about nailing pheasants. What do you think, spit, should I give it a shot?"

But by that point, the spit preferred to keep his mouths shut, which he figured were the same holes as his eyes and ears.

The MACs and the YOCs

The middle-aged couple got in their car in New York City, and drove up to their second home in a coastal town in Massachusetts, whose name did not matter, insofar as that it was like other coastal towns, with rocky beaches, turfy vegetation, and salty air.

The middle-aged couple had been unsure if they would be making the trip. It was Memorial Day weekend, and that was the real start of the summer, as all of the magazines, with their "Fun Summer Things To Do" lists, had shouted. The second home had sat unoccupied for almost two months. "We really should go," Mrs. Middle-Aged Couple said. "After all, what is the point of the place if we do not visit it?"

Mr. Middle-Aged Couple, who would have to do all of the driving, knew it was probably easiest to acquiesce. If they went now, they might not have to go until Fourth of July weekend. "Okay, dear," Mr. MAC smoothly put it. "We'll bring those new folding chairs, too. Should be warm enough to sit out on the beach."

The young, over-their-heads couple, lived next door, in the coastal town whose name did not matter. Their home was not their second home. It was their first and only home. Mr. Young, Over-Their-Heads Couple had introduced Mrs. Young, Over-Their-Heads Couple to the coastal town long before they ever thought of making their first and only home there. He had visited the town many times with women who never became Mrs. YOC. Things had a way of not working out. But he hoped they would, someday, and it appeared they might, with Mrs. YOC, but they were as their name suggested, alas (he had once had a Mr. Wise for a calculus teacher, so he knew how matters like these could dovetail.) They fought. It was one-sided. All of the volume came from him, all of the silence from her, and sometimes his eyes would shake—he could feel them—and he'd get dizzy, and he'd wonder if it was possible to die from arguing.

Then he would go upstairs. He would stand in the window at the back of their bedroom and stare at the birds at all of the feeders she had bought, while he was at work, for him, so he could hang them. But he could not hang them. She was much handier. But he told her where he thought he'd like them best, and she hung them while he went back to work, but she hung them incorrectly, or else exactly where he had told her to, though maybe he failed to remember his own directions. No one knew. The mystery was never solved. But eventually the bird feeders were put right, and he looked down at them in the bedroom where he only sometimes slept. It belonged to whoever went to bed first on any given night. That was enough to make Mr. or Mrs. YOC the claimant of the room. For the duration of that evening it was theirs, and theirs alone. Although it was safest not to let things become too dynastic, and relinquish the room after a three or four night run of occupancy. Any more than three nights, and she could feel his moods darken, tighten, and punching the air with his words gave way to punching the walls with his fists. Additional bird feeder controversies ensued, as more (there many styles of feeders, as it turned out, and he wished to try them all) were purchased from the coastal town's one hardware store. It was just down the road, so there were not a lot of excuses she could make, in terms of accessibility and convenience.

He'd watch the cardinals, jays, finches, doves, and sparrows come and go, and two squirrels, who worked in tandem. One would shake a bird feeder, knocking seed onto the ground, and then both would partake of those sunflower spoils, trading off next time on the shaking duties. He watched Mr. and Mrs. MAC, too, when they came up from New York City. Must be nice, he thought. Two homes. He made a joke: I wonder if he ever thinks of leaving her here, so he can have his other place all to himself. It wasn't really a joke, he realized, so much as a caustic thought. He didn't like when he gave himself over to caustic thoughts. They did seem to get along very well though. They had folding chairs, this time, and sat in their backyard, laughing, talking, sometimes, for ten minutes at a clip, and then not talking for just as long, like they could do it either way.

Maybe he should go downstairs and apologize to Mrs. YOC. She'd like that. Then again, she might not think he was being sincere. That was a big theme of hers. Sincerity. Sometimes he'd been as sincere as he'd ever been, and she would not believe him. He thought that was more her issue though. She didn't believe a lot of people.

"Trust," he'd say, "trust. Trust is a real issue with you. Sometimes I think the more sincere I am, the less you want to believe me, because of what that requires. Vulnerability! And you don't do vulnerability!" He was proud of these last two lines. He regarded them as the "clinchers" to his argument.

He tried them again downstairs. Mrs. YOC looked

bemused. She had heard this speech before. It never worked. She decided to make a stand. She challenged him on his need, as she put it, for control. He had his vulnerability clincher, but she had been working on one of her own, little did he know. Maybe it would sound over-poeticized? She worried about that. It probably would, in the context of an ordinary day. And what was this about, anyway? Bird feeders? Well, that's pretty ordinary. But she also knew it was more than that, although it'd probably be difficult explaining as much to an outsider. She was like an outsider, though, in her own way, with him, with them. So did that mean she couldn't explain it to herself? She knew she was prevaricating. Best to simply try her own clincher before dilly-dallying any further.

"You're a usurper of the self," she said, as he looked far more bemused—and sincerely bemused—than she had, just moments before. "You commandeer (he had given her a word-a-day calendar at Christmas) my self. You try to make it your own. You erase the lines that make me me, my outline, and you let all of the me run out onto the ground like so much…so much (this clincher was harder, as it was improvised)…goop. Like so much goop." There. She even stood by clincher number two by repeating it. That would show him.

Well. Was that ever a misfire. What it ended up showing her was how loud he could get, while revealing to him that it was possible to pass out from yelling. The doctors termed it a minor cardiac event. He did not know how any cardiac event could be minor. She had intended to leave him. She was going to do what one of the British sitcoms she watched, alone, on PBS, called "a legger." This meant running away, in great haste, after packing what she could, while he was somewhere else. So, when he was at work, in other words. Leggers were best done in the middle of the night. The more romantic leggers. The ones that had an element of piracy, or something suitably swashbuckling, to them. But that seemed like an oxymoron (she'd have to remember the word-a-day calendar; it might prove very useful in her future life) to her. A romantic legger? Wasn't she running from romance? Although, really, was this romance? It probably had been at some point. Maybe what surplus of romance there was in earlier, happier times went into a rainy day fund, to be borrowed against in harder times, until there was no more. The figures of romance were quiet confusing. She was sure of that, at least.

He came out of his event a changed man. That is what he said, anyway. His behavior backed him up, but, then again, she questioned his sincerity.

"Fear not, my love, fear not," he said, in as heroic—mock heroic?—a voice she had ever heard him muster. "Fear not. As Scrooge came out changed, so have I."

She purposely hung two more new bird feeders in the wrong spot and waited to see his response. She had her phone ready to call 911. She didn't want to be a murderer. She still thought about her legger, but the differences between a standard legger and a murderer's legger were substantial. He kissed her on the head, instead. "I like your way better, truth be told. How happy we are."

She was not happy though. She was terrified. She decided to tell him one night, after she spent the bulk of the late afternoon in front of the big back window of the bedroom, watching Mr. and Mrs. MAC have their annual Fourth of July eve cookout in their backyard. They never socialized much with them. There was quite an age gap. He liked to say—before his minor event—that you're as fit and fresh as the company you kept. He said it like he was the inventor of the phrase, but his father said it, too, and who knows how many fathers before that.

"Yes," she would tell him. She was happy for him, that he had changed—if this were true; she could not relinquish her doubts—but, even still, things were not working. She would catch him by surprise. Then his true nature would announce itself. He wouldn't be able to keep it in check. But even if he did, well, there was that sincerity issue of his. People don't just change. Not like that. Scrooge was an aberration. Besides, that was his favorite film. Of course he'd want to…commandeer it… like that. How convenient. Too convenient.

"It's behavioral, more than anything," he offered. "One can change one's behavior. It's much less dramatic, much less involved, than you would have it. My love." He bought her a Paul McCartney CD. "This makes me think of you, now," he said. "The more sublime songs. Which is to say, the ones with love at their core."

This was too much. He used to say he liked Lennon far more than McCartney, because the latter was "soft" and the former was "hard." He even told her a story—she figured it was apocryphal (she could not deny him the efficacy in his choice of dictionaries…most people buy ones with puppies or lighthouses, like he used to, so she'd have to give him points there)—in which John Lennon stood on top of a house and urinated on the heads of nuns. He seemed proud of Lennon for this. Certainly not critical, anyway.

But now it was time to move. Time to get out from

this window and tell him how she felt. She was moving to do so when she caught sight of him waving at her. He was in the backyard of Mr. and Mrs. MAC, with a sparkler in his hand. The MACs were folding up their lawn chairs, and heading inside. He kept waving, doing that pulling wave which means you want someone to follow you. A beckoning wave.

She didn't have a chance to say anything once she got outside. He was very fast. "Come inside, love. We've been invited." He spoke more candidly than she ever heard him speak before. She could not believe the things he was saying, and to strangers. "What is the secret to your love," he asked, while playing cribbage. "Do you believe love is cyclical? That is, that one person pulls the sled more than the other, during a given interval, as the other person will, later on?"

She was embarrassed for him. The more wine he drank, the more questions there were, but she knew what he would say, if pressed on that: it wasn't the wine that led to more questions, but the passing of time. Oh, he was a sly one. Mrs. MAC smiled a lot. She was touched. For years she'd known how Mr. MAC had tired of her. Not that this was horrible. He bore her no ill will, for the most part. But he was older, and where once there had been passion, as the young people put it, now there was something more…

"Quotidian," Mrs. YOC offered, as they cut slices of apple pie in the kitchen, and heaped them with vanilla ice cream, while the men sat in the drawing room.

"Look…I'm not trying to be rude, but I popped a couple Viagra because we really weren't expecting any company tonight, and unless you're swingers I need to ask you to leave and give us some privacy. It's rude barging in like that. Only my wife is too polite not to say so."

Mr. YOC figured that Mr. MAC might have been a John Lennon fan. They ate hurriedly, and left with valedictions of "we'll have to do this again, and soon."

Mrs. YOC put aside her legger, for the time being, although she figured it was always an option, and would probably always be a viable one. She waited for her husband to reveal himself, but damn, could he fake it. Years went by before she realized that every day had been a legger, but of the quietest, least swashbuckling variety.

"Can you pack up, and run from yourself," she asked herself, in her thoughts. When he did not break in on them, while they sat there at the breakfast table, on the latest Sunday, drinking coffee, she worried that he should have, like he could pick up on what was happening in these most delicate moments, and should have intervened to show her how much he cared, how sincere he was about there being no goop.

"What would you like to do today, love? Maybe we could say hello to the new couple next door."

He'd been leery about this subject. The police tape had only come down a couple months ago. No foul play had been proven. A school boy had confessed to the broken window. Mrs. MAC was in NYC. They tended to spend more time in separate houses. By then, Mr. and Mrs. YOC had a second home in the city, and missed most of the excitement.

"That would be..." She searched through her mind for a suitably impressive word, even though he had returned to giving her calendars that featured puppies and light houses. He didn't like when she didn't sound like herself.

"That would be...nice."

He smiled. "Nice it is, then, love, nice it is."

Blue Crystals

When Doze returned from the war, he decided he'd wait a bit before visiting his garage. He wasn't sure, exactly, what war he'd been in, but the general consensus in the town was that he'd been in battle, and acquitted himself, more or less, well. Or, at least, not poorly.

This confused Doze; after all, if a man made it out, and he had not acted cowardly, how could there be any debate as to how well or not so well he had done? And why hadn't the same people who were discussing his performance, and its merits, not been alongside to have seen for themselves?

Some of them, he figured, probably had. There was a good deal of murk in those early moments, upon returning home. Doze himself was amazed that he could resist his garage. He didn't think he had that kind of self-discipline. Still, as he thought about his various battle scenes, he began to feel that maybe his fellow citizens—even the rowdier guys from the rotary club, who loved to give him the business, as they put it—weren't to be faulted for wondering—and wondering aloud; which may have been better, or it may have been worse, he wasn't sure—about the specifics of his ordeals. He concluded that he'd probably do the same thing, if he were one of them, and one of them had been where he had been, though where that was, he couldn't really tell, just then, because of the murk. But the murk would probably subside, and life, once more, would settle into a routine, because that is what life does.

He was pretty sure that he had been a science teacher for many years. There was no doubt that he had been one, at least for some. Because there was his garage. And that bad, nasty joke that people used to make about his wife. The boys and girls of the town probably had been doing what many of them, from time to time, did before he went away, with their baseball bats, the shovels from their father's garages, bricks they toted along in backpacks, and even fruit, although fruit, of course, was never going to work. That's what they thought. Doze, naturally, knew better. A good orange, with all of that juice, all of that sweet acidity, could make a go of it. But that was the riddle: you had to know that something more than brawn, and force, was required.

Not that he had set it up as a riddle. He cast his memory back on those days as he walked through the school. No one was there, except a woman at the front desk. She got on the phone when she saw him. It was nice for a member of the staff to be so casual in front of him, and not standing on ceremony, treating him like he had never left, and was, instead, perhaps, running back from his car to get his briefcase, which he tended to forget. The lucky days were the days he remembered to retrieve his briefcase before he got halfway home. Failing to do so wouldn't sit well with his wife. He remembered how sick she had been. And that he was a science teacher; one who won awards, and was not infrequently written up in the local papers, and even, sometimes, papers from surrounding towns, and once from a different state.

He hoped the woman at the desk didn't see the look on his face that he assumed she would mistake for arrogance. It wasn't that he was arrogant, or very prideful;

still, it felt nice to feel proud, and what man didn't have the right, from time to time, to enjoy just how good he had been at something. That was fine, that was fitting. But maybe that's why people questioned, aloud, or to themselves, what he had done during his battles, and how well, or poorly, he had done it. He had the sense that they all wanted it to be one or the other. A mediocre performance, a typical performance, would not have worked as well. So very humdrum, one of the rotary club men would say; or not say, at all, aloud. So very humdrum. It was like he could hear that voice—Parker would be its owner—as he walked through the halls of the school, like Parker had become the principal, and was making announcements over the intercom. But they were very personal announcements, in this case, and Doze would have to make a note to voice his displeasure later, at the right time.

There was a skeleton in his old classroom. They didn't have that before. He hoped that the new teacher did not make ghoulish jokes. He probably had enough to contend with, when someone raised their hand, and asked about Doze's garage. Those crystals. The crystals he grew, first in his basement, and then outside, in the backyard, until a ring of blue went around the edges of his lawn, making it look like a sea of mint, outlined by ice. This couldn't be his wife though. Probably. She wouldn't have been here, in his old classroom. It was wrong, he decided—knowing he'd probably reverse himself later in the day, as was his custom (and the murk wasn't helping, to be honest)—to joke as they did. Like she was in there. In that garage, covered in blue crystal, that he grew and grew and grew, with no one to see him doing so, even

24

though, with Doze being a kind of small town phenom-
enon, kids tried to catch him at all hours of the day and
night.

Sure, he uttered a few gentle remonstrances when
the children first arrived with their bats, shovels, and
bricks, but whack away if you must, whack away, he'd say.
Those garage walls were virtually petrified, and thick,
too. Several feet thick, shiny and engorged and so hard
you could hardly chip them. The children would sing,
and not just when they were at Doze's garage, but other
times, too, with their friends, if they wanted to annoy
them, or frighten them. *Doze, Doze, nobody knows.* He
knew, anyway, that what they did not know, and what the
song referenced, was what was on the inside of Doze's garage. He didn't know either. Or, rather, he had, he felt, but
then there was all the murk, and so much war to contend
with. To say nothing about the PR side of the war, post-
war, when everyone wondered what his role had been,
and how well, or not so well, he had done it.

He prepared to leave the school, taking one last
stroll, for the time being, through the halls, peeking into
the empty classrooms, trying to decide when he'd re-ap-
ply for his post, hoping that the new teacher could be
kept on staff, too. Maybe he had an interest in crystals
and crystal growing, and they could pool their ideas, and
their resources, and make a club of sorts. The rotary guys
wouldn't want to participate; they never did; but that was
fine, and, all in all, for the best. It was a wise idea to have
separate groups, and separate groups of friends. That way,
a man could feel truly balanced in his life, and versatile.
Balanced. That's the enemy of murk, he thought, and was
proud—and indulged himself in the feeling; after all, he'd

been through a lot, no matter what anyone said—that he had coined an aphorism, or something that could, over time, with a little work, and some tinkering, become an aphorism that he might say aloud to people someday—starting with his students—and maybe they'd think well enough of it to say it themselves, to other people. Science is a great conductor. And there was another one. Doze, who did not normally use sports expressions, decided that he was on fire.

He forgot his briefcase, of course. Isn't that always the way? When he rushed back, past the now empty check-in desk, he realized that he hadn't brought it at all with him that day, but he took a look around his classroom all the same, and walked over to the skeleton. A fine specimen. Even though the bones had been artificially whitened. He dropped down to his knees and stared up through the hole in the pelvis, with the bottom of his eyelid flush against the bone. No, it was not his wife, he was pretty sure. The space in back of the hole wasn't like he figured the space in the back of the hole in her pelvis would be like. Oh well. There's that variety again, he thought, and he could feel his new aphorism paying significant thematic dividends already.

It was dark when he finally got to his garage. He didn't think there would be any kids out tonight, given how long he'd been gone. Then again, word in the town probably traveled fast, and kids could be impressively opportunistic. Reflected swaths of blue moonlight lit up the base of Doze's petrified garage. There were bats, shovels, and bricks all around. He got on his knees again, and started running his hands along the ground, in the darkness, to see if there were any stray bits of crystal, that would cut him, and make him bleed. The crystal would have had that effect, he surmised, even though no one, not even himself, had ever managed to break any of it. But his hands remained dry, and unscathed, so now it was time.

He worked for many hours. He did not know how many, but it remained dark, so it wouldn't have been for as long as he felt like he was working. Piles of orange skins grew on all sides of Doze's garage, as he rubbed the fruit into the blue crystal, dissolving it, layer by layer. Eventually, on the back wall, where he worked the longest, as it provided him with cover from the street, he got down to the wood. Not a lot of wood, but enough for a man to squeeze himself through, if he was desperate enough, and didn't mind a few splinters. That is, once the wood had been kicked in, as Doze had just done.

The inside of the garage was very small. He'd forgotten just how much the crystal had added, from the standpoint of visual heft. Crystal was like that; distorting. But in a cleaner, shinier way than the murk. He laughed, because of course his wife wasn't in there. And the green piece of paper, that was outlined in a thin, icing-like layer of crystal, was so much like his lawn that he couldn't wait to pick it up, because wouldn't it be something if you could hold your backyard in your hand, like a child holds a top. Maybe the new science teacher was also a budding aphorism buff, and could help him incorporate this found text into something that would please them both. *I did because you did.* Still, individuality ought to be valued. He would try that one, too, if given the opportunity, at the rotary club.

Ribbons

He thought he'd try something daring, this time, upon entering the house. Something to show the quality of his spirit, which he felt was brightening by the day, and becoming more agile, too, as was his mind. That'd show her. How she'd love it. Wouldn't know what to make of this latest form of his, especially as each of his forms were always so indelible. You'd be challenged to think so many forms could exist in a single man, and with this latest, well, what recourse would she have but to partake in everything he offered her, at the level of her own individual level, of course. That was his thing: anyone could find themselves in what he had to offer, or a place for them to belong and subsist, for that was how he operated. On many levels at once. He chuckled. "A place for the groundlings, and the scholars. That is what I provide. Your level is your own business. But there's always one for you here."

By "here" he meant within the range of his mind, and whatever you were fortunate enough to have him teach you. The door, a mere formality; he was such a frequent visitor at this point that he felt no compunction in not knocking, instead sliding into the front hall, gracefully, like he'd just stepped out of *Singin' in the Rain*, a film which he could expound on with the most dogged of cinephiles. What would she be wearing? An odd thought. Hadn't had many of those, of late. In the early days, sure. She'd be humming a pop song, in a loose fitting-blouse, or a t-shirt without a bra. That had been all right. Distracting, but all right all the same. He was a professional. But too many t-shirts-without-bras incidents, back then, had the effect of turning his mind up at its corners—before he had fully mastered it, that is to say—and dicey, dangerous thoughts replaced his usual informed, controlled ones.

"Maybe ask her to slip into a bikini. Can we do that? Hmmm. Maybe make it this sort of Brigitte Bardot thing. Could talk to her about burgeoning female sexuality in the pre-code films of the 1930s. Such atavistic films. There'd be wetness then. Could see about sliding right in."

But then he would fight to make his way back to the core of his mind, and all the good order and logic that reigned there. Plus, there was the time factor. One only lived for so long. Best to stay focused. To say nothing of her husband. They'd not really met. Not formally. He didn't believe they'd "ingratiate well," as he put it to her. Besides, the husband was the distant sort. Off doing whatever he did. An overblown sense of self worth, clearly.

Still, most of the other husbands of the world—or the state, or of that town, anyway—probably would have envied him. Quite base, but they would have envied him all the same. The t-shirt/brains combo would have done it. There was no denying that she had the latter. That's why he was so generous with his time. She was generous, too, in her own ways. Gave him a sweater for his birthday not too long back. She always remembered his birthday. He had a devil of a time recalling hers, but, then again, that was not what he had signed on for, or, to get technical about it, what anyone asked of him.

He had his duties, and he tended to them in a manner that he felt—though he did not regard himself as a

29

prideful man—as matchless. The last sweater framed his paunch. That was unbecoming. Naturally, he realized that she had picked up on the worried look that must have darkened his face. He felt it. Ah, a rigid left cheek. Will give you away every time. But he could joke. He'd tell her, often, that he could joke, and he'd joke more in the future, maybe, when there was more time.

He'd made a great discovery about time one day, when they had occasion to run an errand together. He worked with her so regularly that sometimes it was easier to "take the lesson on the road," as he put it, if there was one that simply could not keep. She had a lot of errands to tend to. Trips to the cleaners with the husband's clothes; trips to the grocery store with long lists of foodstuffs the husband liked; stops at the deluxe spirits shop that stocked the fine single malt whiskies the husband preferred. But yes, his joke. He said the words slowly, when he made it, enunciating each of them in that faintly British way of his, which he maintained was not a matter of affectation, but instead a result of proper diction, something which he always extolled to her.

"It's a framer. It frames my paunch."

She laughed at him, like he was so ridiculous to have any doubts as to the suavity of his appearance, like any woman could. He disagreed with her on this score (just as he liked how often she had begun using that phrase, further proof that his influence was seeping through her calcified, outer layer, after all of these years), but clearly she believed what she said, just as he noticed that what she said had as much to do with the way she said it, as with the words she used. "There is a dearth of artifice there," he concluded, confused that she'd been able to speak so clearly while not, technically, speaking so clearly, but he figured more information on the subject would probably occur to him later, for that is how he felt that everything in his life went. "If I need to know, if I truly need to know, something will make me aware of it." There was a comfort in knowing that he had a most generous intellectual benefactor somewhere out there, amongst the muses.

So in he slid, like he'd come from *Singin' in the Rain.* Today, he would be imparting his wisdom on Wagner's Ring cycle and how it was both classical and postmodern at once, a point he was fairly certain no one had made before. Just as the weekend prior he had made the argument—most successfully—that the Beatles' "A Day in the Life" and "A Hard Day's Night" were the same song, more or less, structurally, although no one would have thought to equate them. "Pop and rock. Twined. Not conflated, not concatenated. But rather twined. Do you understand?"

"Tutee!" he shouted, as he slid. "Oh, tutee!" She'd like the new nickname, which would do until his chimerical spirit, with its penchant for mutability, thought up another, which would, again, blow her mind. She did not come out right away. That was a growing trend. It annoyed him. Especially given his recent discovery on the nature of time. Outside of your head, time ruled you. It was the stronger force. There was nothing you could do about that. Time wasn't going to have an off-day. Not so much as an off-second. But inside your head, you could compact time. That is, you could superimpose your thoughts, such that they weren't happening sequentially, as everything, more or less, took place on the outside. Sure, you could multitask, as he told her, but even if you could do twenty things at once, in your head you could do as many as your intellect would allow. So you could do like 200.

She was a flash in the bedroom doorway. She always came out of the bedroom doorway. It was on the first floor, so he felt it probably was not the most intimate of bedrooms. His eye caught sight of a red ribbon. He thought it was a ribbon, although it was bright enough that it seemed almost electric, rather than a piece of fabric, or cloth, or whatever ribbons are made of. But it was more blurry than anything. He didn't like to waste time with chit-chat, but the ribbon-type entity gained a foothold in his imitation.

"What was that?"

"Who was that, you mean."

"There is no time for games."

"That was my husband."

He'd play along. Maybe she was trying to con him into a liaison, and this was how she'd get him into the bedroom. He had remarked to her several times that curiosity was his tragic flaw, insofar as he had one.

"He's here today?"

"Yes. Today he is here. Very busy."

Confounding. The lessons resumed. He could feel her growing, even if she looked darker, tighter, drier around the edges. Like a piece of paper left out in the sun. But she performed admirably. Enough so that her old manner of expression was almost totally gone now. How he had winced back when she would use a word like "dude." Anti-euphonious. There were less loose-fitting blouse and braless t-shirt displays, and if she hummed anything it was an aria that he was apt to hum as well, not pop songs anymore, and he wondered when the day would arrive where they'd break into a humming duet, after which they'd share a well-earned laugh.

She'd come out of the bedroom to greet him, and he'd always look for a glimpse of the ribbon, so as to ascertain what it truly was. Sometimes he'd take the initiative.

"I thought I might talk to your husband," he said. "Try to feel him out. Inform him of your progress."

"Don't you think that would be strange?"

"Well, if he's too busy, I guess he's too busy."

"I am sure he's too busy."

"Fair enough. Now, for some learning."

There were years of learning. He assumed that she must have discussed making the arrangement permanent with her husband. What a gig! She learned faster and faster all the time, until it was like she had been programmed by the same muses whom he believed plied him with his stores of knowledge. She still made the joke about her husband in the bedroom, and he still played along. Indulging her seemed to help get them into each day's lesson faster.

But then he came to the day when the door did not open for him, on his own, and he was not able to slide into the hallway, near where the bedroom was, like he'd just come from *Singin' in the Rain*. It was unlike her to commit a scheduling gaffe; in fact, in all of those years, it was the first such example, so there was nothing to do but try and be the bigger person and be forgiving. He'd show up the next day, and not dwell on it for more than five minutes, thus making his point, economically, and showing how kind he could be.

But the next day produced the same result, and the next day, too, and the day after that. Without his gig, he found himself desperate. And daring. He put on the sweater she gave him. It was a dark sweater. Perfect for the night. He had some black slacks. She had also given him them. It was time to be a cuss. She had driven him to it. In the night, he blended in with the fire escape. He hopped up on the first platform. Maybe he could have been a diamond thief. The bedroom window was open. This was easy enough. Odd.

Even his imagination could not have conceived of a darker room. It was like being in an underground closet. He did not know what or whom he'd chance upon, but if it was time to lay on, he was prepared to lay on.

He searched that room for years, every evening. Something sent—certified mail, he joked, darkly—from the muses told him to. Prowling, prying, investigating, tapping floorboards, tapping walls. There was no bed, no furniture, no anything, but the room struck him as a most complex room, nonetheless. He'd read that powders could be a great aid in deductive matters. You could take some and throw it up in the air, and when it came down it'd blanket the surface you were investigating such that you'd be able to see signs and lettering and clues that you'd not been able to see before. So he got some powder and set to work. And lo, two snakes, dead, in the middle of the room. He touched them with his foot. Maybe they weren't snakes at all. It was time to be brave. He held the forms in the moonlight, by the window, and blew as hard as he could. Two ribbons, one red, another that had been blue—he was able to isolate trace fiber strands under the microscope that he had taken to carrying around with him—that was now choked with bright, angry hues of red.

"Well, muses?" he asked, and waited, and waited, and waited. "Well?"

"Give him some time," one of the muses said to one of his mates. "No point in sending him anything just yet. We could go for a beer."

"A long beer?"

"Sure. We have time. He's not going anywhere."

The Hagfish

He considered it beneath him, frankly: twisting into a knot, for the purpose of entering into the latest dead carcass that had drifted down from the surface, where the sunlight was, so as to eat his way out. What a way to subsist. His contemporaries had no problem with it, and there they'd be, day after day, contorting themselves and passing into a bloated tuna fish, or a chunky seal, and even the occasional felled shark, although he suspected, when a shark did make it down to "the grounds"—for that is what he always called the reef where he lived, even though no one else did—that the shark had died of natural causes.

He knew some lampreys who tagged along with many sharks in their careers, but they tended to be idiots, and heavy drinkers besides. Leave it to a lamprey to get high on salt water. It probably had something to do with the rotted flesh that was always around their mouths. That made sense. There'd once been a man who drifted down to the grounds, and he could tell, sure enough, that the man had been drinking the same water that the lampreys would drink, only without their level of sense, as he obviously had overindulged to a more dangerous degree.

What a pain it was contorting himself into the man and eating him from the inside out, but he was especially bored in those days, and exhibited, it was said, a self-destructive streak. True, it was a duty of sorts, for him to consume the man as he did, and he was aware of some of his comrades—although he thought the label far too generous—watching him from inside of the creatures they were presently inhabiting, and devouring.

They'd always eat the eyes out first, so they could look through those holes at whatever he was doing. Wit was not, exactly, a common staple of the grounds, but this was one of the better examples, and he'd think, Christ Almighty. Idiots. If you can't come up with some new material, maybe make a modicum of effort to better yourself. By this point, he'd have torn fifteen or so strips of flesh from whatever he was inside of, and he could tell that his own mucus had commingled with the flesh to the point that no possible joy could be derived from this meal, even if he were eating it in better circumstances, which he felt was, if not his birthright, then at least something he could aspire to, or dream about.

When he put the matter to his fellow hagfish, they stared at him mutely, as they always did. He had tried to initiate an activities club in which, from week to week, a given pursuit would be selected—say, trying to better understand the hermit crabs who, for so long, had governed themselves without any input from anyone, or seeing who could compose the best song by beating on the water with his barbels. The winner would be the composer who made his sound waves go all the way to the surface—although this would be difficult to gauge—but the mere mention of this surface would cause the other hagfish to start discussing what their next meal would be. Not that they had any control over it, and when he tried to point this out, there'd always be this questioning voice that would bring up the time when one of them—at a similar activities meeting—had expressed a desire to coil himself up in a seagull, and eat his way through the bird.

Wouldn't it be the way, then, that a seagull, only a few hours later, came floating down to the grounds. He knew how difficult it would be to convince his would-be activity partners that this was mere happenstance, and not the same thing as placing an order. But then three more gulls followed, but he kept his mouth shut—the epidemic talk, he believed, would get him nowhere—until he reluctantly joined in the dinner, because, after all, he had his strength to think of, given that he had big plans in mind.

They were not the most solid of plans, but then again, he was not the most solid of creatures, given his body type, a joke which he was proud of, and shared with his fellows, who were curled up in the hollows of the reef, sucking on their own mucus. This was just soulless. He began to rail, stating that they had been equipped, nobly, with the slime they all shared—he thought this a most effective speech-making technique, bridging the distance between speaker and audience—to clog the gills of their enemies, who would, in following, be forced to spit them out, just as he had once observed—on his own, since no one else would join that particular activity group—an octopus spit out a hermit crab who had placed a sea anemone on his head. Sea anemones were not tasty to octopi. He almost lost it when one of the others said that the hermit crab probably just wanted a decorative hat, and that hermit crabs were very vain.

So it went for years and years, and he felt like he parted with a portion of who he was, or who he could have been, anyway, each time he felt the eyes on him, from the insides of various animals—there had even been a horse, and a cobra, but no one would go inside the cobra, because that felt vaguely incestuous, and they weren't sure—even he wasn't sure—if the cobra was a drowned cousin of theirs. So they let the lobsters have him, lest they be brought bad luck, or, worse, became cursed. The cobra signaled some darks times on the grounds. That was how he put it, pleased with the double-meaning on the word dark, because it was, in one sense, always dark where they lived, but there had been talk—well, he had talked—about making an exploratory trip to the surface, to where the beams of light were.

He was laughed at, of course, and some of the older, supposedly wiser, hagfish told him that those beams were cousins of the hagfish, why, look at their shape. And if he was going up to the surface to try and contort himself and eat his cousins from the inside out, he best forget about it, because he'd bring ruin on all of them, for there was a natural give and take, in these matters, between cousins, good and evil, and the surface and the grounds. No matter how desirous you become for a greater variety of food, they cautioned. And when he'd say food had nothing to do with it, was the furthest thing from his mind, he'd be chided for not being grateful that more humans, and gulls, and a barracuda—again, he assumed this was a case of natural causes—had lately floated down to them.

What a grind it was to eat his way out of something, every day. He decided to enact what was tantamount to a hunger strike, although he knew that the others would think he was playing at some sort of game they didn't understand. Instead of eating anything from the inside out, he sunk his teeth into the outside of the latest corpse, and then pulled back his jaws, and attempted to set his teeth down in the exact grooves that he had just made. Rarely did teeth and groove tally, but the sight of him floating downwards, his quarry beside him, and his head and jaws moving towards it, and back again, over and over, made everyone else question his motives, to say nothing of his sanity. Maybe he was a showboater now, and there was talk that the hermit crabs—with their ostentatious hats—were starting to take notice, as though they might, in an unprecedented move, welcome him into their fold.

But the game did not prove satisfying, and before too long—which is to say, after several years of trying to perfect it—he knew that all that was left to him was above him, in those rays of light, near the surface. No one, naturally, went to the surface, so it was with much to-do—and after a number of lengthy meetings, and interventions, with his fellow hagfish (for even those who did not care one jot about him, were worried about what curses he might instigate, and then those rays of light would be everyone's problem) —that the community gathered at the edge of the grounds, at the top of the reef, and watched him float, and float, and float, snapping his tail as powerfully as he could, to the surface, where, inevitably, they lost sight of him.

He swam just barely underwater for several days, trying to screw up his courage, and deliberating whether it really was a good idea to attempt and contort himself into a shape like the fist that humans had, and get inside one of those rays of light. To date, he'd been dodging them, lithely moving left or right, so as not to even risk bumping into one. When a large, floating contraption, which was brown, and much lighter than he was, came into view, and then passed over his head, so close that he could see a spinning mechanism at the back of it, he decided that if ever there was a sign that now was the time, this was it, for the mechanism at the back had a shape like the coiled one he made when it was necessary to get inside of something.

And just as he made that shape, and passed into a ray of light, he could feel the difference. The slime that had covered his body for so many years began to float away in the water, and he became shorter, and shorter, and his tale sharper, and sharper. The light had taken him into the mechanism that was shaped like he sometimes was, and the sensation was most curious. His tail felt like it had become chiseled and pointed, and when he looked back, through the water that was now red, like the insides of so many things he had once seen, he was able to confirm this was so.

Never did he think that he could travel as rapidly as he did now, like he was some spike falling through the water, down to the grounds. A trail of red streaked behind him, and he saw the faces of the others as he ripped past them. It was good to give them all a start, he thought, as he hit the silt below the reef, and the hermit crabs advanced, to see what the surface had so generously provided them with this time.

The Glazier's Art

For years he'd sit nights in the window at the top of his house, looking at the salt crystals that stuck to the glass. In the morning, he'd wipe them away again, but he knew that the sea would provide, in this matter, if not in others, as he figured his father would have said, if he had a father, but he hadn't, he'd just been there all along.

That was the neat thing about him, in his mind. On some nights he would play games with the crystals, trying to guess which constellations they were attempting to imitate in the various shapes they made. Pavo was a popular constellation shape of late, and he thought this quite clever of the crystals and the sea wind that helped arrange them, because Pavo was Latin for peacock, and how he would have liked to show off what he had discovered, for he thought few men would have had the patience and creativity to have done so.

But then Pavo went away, and there was a prosaic run of Dippers and Orion and Sagittarius. That lot. All the boring ones, you might say, like the crystals had lost their edges. The glass could be very giving though, and of a most mercurial temperament, and so he stared harder, remembering the time he'd read a story about a man who kept looking at an old tintype, and how the people in the tintype would move, from day to day. The man wouldn't see them move, of course. They had to be subtle about it. But he remembered where they had been before, and he noted that they were no longer there. It was dead exciting. So much so that that man asked a collegial friend of his to observe with him, and he saw it too. The past was trying to tell them something, they decided. About them? No, that wasn't it. About someone who had been wrongfully accused of something and then was killed but made to look like he had committed suicide. It was quite black. A lot of things were back then. Tintypes came from another era. But glass was a constant. Glass was a survivor. So he looked harder and harder at the glass in his window, waiting for what would come next, for the latest game, or, better yet, maybe a revelation that would come in the form of a game, or, who knows, perhaps something along the lines of the tintype drama, but in glass instead.

The streetlights didn't help. They shone on the glass, and, he felt, compromised its integrity, so he acquired the services of a ladder from a shifty Irishman he knew, who had made nontraditional use of the tool. He wouldn't say anything further. Which was odd, because the shifty Irishman, with the shifty name, normally was highly voluble. Actually, was that true? He'd run off at the mouth a lot. That was true. With his fancy words. But other times he was as vocal as a slug, even as his eyes were darting about like some bird that could not wait to find and tear the head off of a—what did birds eat? A mouse. Or something more substantial. Like a gopher.

"What do you want it for then? Machinations?"

"No, Mr. Padraig."

"I told you. It's Padraig. And, when we are being conspiratorial like this, it's P."

"Okay. Mr. P. I need it for my glass. I think I might see something in it if I can cut out the lights."

"That's the trick of it, isn't it? Boyo."

He liked when P would call him boyo. It sounded

so distinguished, like a great honor had been conferred upon him. Mr. P was the local criminal. He'd written a memoir. A dossier of gentlemanly crimes. They met at the bookstore. There was but twelve stores in the town. Most of them sold lobster traps. Mr. P had given a grave reading to the men who bought the lobster traps. There were candles lighting the reading room, and they played well against the bookstore's glass, he thought, and began working up ideas for experiments back in his primary watching room, where the salt crystals played at their games of shapes, while still listening to Mr. P's reading, lest he be rude.

"My ladder for you, Doze, my ladder for you. May it serve you better than it has, to date, served me. Where the fuck did you get a name like that, anyway?"

"Family name."

"Like you come from a long line of sleepers?"

He laughed. He knew that Mr. P wasn't trying to be funny, but you had to be leery with criminals, and observe the proper social cues.

That night he lost some glass time, because he had underestimated how many street lamps there were. He'd lean the ladder against one of the lamp poles, shimmy up to the top part when the ladder wouldn't go any further, and throw one of his obsidian-black bath towels over the lamp.

The bath towels were something of a misfire. He got them after she left. Or, rather, after he made her leave, but not on purpose. It was tricky. Complicated. The therapist he spoke to did not understand, and how he longed to be as articulate as Mr. P, and even thought about bringing him along to one of his sessions, as an interpreter, sort of, but a criminal would never do in that arena, and besides, everyone knew—including the therapist, who lived several houses down the road—that Mr. P had discovered, with his ladder, a toe, in or around his domicile, and it was not certain whether Mr. P had planted the toe there, to bolster his own legend as a brigand, or whether he had sliced it off someone who had come to their town, and then left, abruptly.

The therapist had been more helpful with the masturbation problem, and the shame it produced, working away at himself to the thought of her, with another man, like the man she'd been with, twice, before she met him, that she had met that same night. A ghastly mistake, she called it. So out of character. She had put the condom on. He wanted to know. Or, rather, he was hoping that she hadn't, like she was less of an expert in these matters, but she even knew to squeeze the tip. Disgusted as he was at the time, the image had gotten the better of him after she was gone, and he used it, frequently, so frequently that there had been complaints that the wives of the men with the lobster traps had caught sight of him abusing himself in the window where he observed the crystals and sought most forms of his entertainment. The therapist had suggested he switch to black towels to replace the white ones he had been using, so the evidence of his shame could stare him right back in the face. "A fitting juxtaposition," the therapist said, "a fitting juxtaposition. You cannot fail to notice."

He thought he had removed all of the light, and was now free to see what the glass was up to, but each time he raced back inside, and ran up the steps, and got on his knees—for such a delicate matter required the closest of inspections—he'd notice additional glare, and his head would turn in the direction of what he figured it was its source, and then he'd find another lamppost, like it had sprung up in the interval between throwing the towel over the last one and the time it took him to get back upstairs. Days went by. The lampposts, and their lights, only made themselves known at night, and it took some doing to ferret them all out. And even when, finally, he detected no glare, he decided to wait another night, just in case there was some psychological game at play, and the lampposts were trying to "psyche him out," as the kids put it.

One night gave way to another, and eventually he accepted that his victory over the lampposts was complete. Other generations of lampposts might come along to avenge their forefathers, but that was not a concern of his at the moment. He could detect no salt grains in the glass. They must have been there though. The wind would come up from the sea, all in a tizzy, and understandably so, as it was chocked with salt, and that salt had to be deposited somewhere. So he lost one game, but he was confident that the glass would provide, and sure enough, after several months, it did, and his patience was rewarded.

There was a house across the street. He had noticed it, off and on, over the years. Sometimes, before she had left, she had walked over to it. For visiting, she said. He could see her, fleetingly, but that could be distracting, so he tried to maintain his focus. The house went in and out of his mind. Some days, it was there, all white, like his towels used to be, with a picket fence, also white. A historical home. From the 1840s. But all of the homes of the town were like that, including the one that Mr. P occupied on occasion, when he had regional business.

But now the glass wanted him to see something beyond the house, something he was sure was undetectable without the glass's aid. True, this was not the same as the tintype effect, but maybe it was better, because the glass would show you things that you couldn't see without it, and what he saw was a fence that was made out of cedar wood, and covered in creepers, vines, and gray lichens that stood out against the rose-wood coloring. He wondered if the lichens ate the wood, and that was why they were there.

This fence did not demarcate one yard from another. It was too short, only seven or eight feet long. The birds that the glass were now showing him wouldn't go near it. Nor would the squirrels who went near everything, even the undersides of cars, where they were mashed. He had thought about skinning one of them back when he was battling the lampposts, and seeing if the hide would block out the light, but that would have required a lot of squirrels, and he didn't have all day to try and gather that many pelts. The glass seemed (rarely was anything announced outright in their relationship) to want him to know that there was something bewitching behind that cedar fence, with the lichens eating away at it.

Day by day the beard of creepers, vines, and lichens grew thicker, shaggier, and he assumed, now, that birds would start building their nests in that vegetal mess, but no matter how much he pressed his face up against the glass, so that he was re-breathing his own breath as it bounced back to him off of the window, he could see no evidence of anything that flew. But there were creatures who walked. He had not really noticed his neighbors before, thinking that neighbors lived on the same side of the street as you, and these people were across the street, at a completely different latitude. Which had to make them foreigners. The therapist disagreed, as his wife once had. Mr. P, at least, took up the argument, saying that all proverbial neighbors were but foreigners, for who can we really know, when so few of us—nay, none of us—truly know ourselves. But then again, Mr. P was very wise, and wise men were often impractical, and that is probably why Mr. P. was a criminal, albeit one who penned a practical memoir. Life was so confusing away from the glass. There was no denying it. Let others try, he thought, let others try.

He would never call the glass confusing, but it could be quirky, and that's what he decided it was as he watched the people—he decided to be progressive in his thinking, and call them neighbors—walk out to the cedar fence in the evening.

Sometimes, it was just one of them. The man who was probably his age. Or the woman, who was probably younger than his wife had been, when he forced her to move without trying to. The man would occasionally go back into the house, and bring his wife out with him, and they'd both go behind the fence. Afterwards, they'd stand there for a while, apparently in deep thought. Hands would be pressed to chins, shoulders would be shrugged. Then they'd go back around again, and emerge, redoubling their pressing and shrugging efforts.

This went on for longer than he could tell. The glass was so fascinating, with this latest game—which was like a parlor mystery—that he just about forgot what a clock was for. One night, he saw Mr. P., and, to his amazement, the criminal walked right into his neighbors' yard, heading for the cedar fence. He was sly about it, and moved quickly, but Mr. P. always went about like that, even if he was doing something normal and indicative of being a good citizen, like buying a pickle at the country store, and cutting it up with a knife and throwing it into the sea so that the crabs could have something different to nibble on. He felt guilty that he never fed the crabs. The glass enjoyed Windex, and he fed it plenty, and the more he fed it, the more he asked it why it couldn't get him into his neighbors' yard, so that he could see what was behind the fence. It wasn't that he was a bird, and would be in violation of what appeared to be their avian code of conduct. No Cedar Wall. He would have respected that code. That's the kind of person he had become, ever since he had forced her to leave without meaning to.

One night though—he just couldn't take the suspense anymore—he broke all protocol, and threw open the window, no doubt dislodging the salt crystals that he could no longer see. Maybe they had been leaving him messages, in a new code for him to crack, rather than constellation shapes, but that was a risk he felt he had to take in his fence-based surveillance. The window was the best, purest way to go, but he backed away from it at the last moment, shut it again, and went downstairs, to try the door. He got as far as his neighbor's driveway, but no further. His manner of egress probably had something to do with it. A door will only let you get so far, when you've sided with a window, as he had.

So he slept on the matter. For what must have been several days, or a good many moments, anyway. But, thankfully, to his great relief, he awoke buoyed by answers. He liked that his mind kept working even when his body shut down. To the hardware store he went, to buy replacement glass. It was a bold decision, to throw himself through the glass that was already there, but he remembered reading that the only way out was through, and he was a skilled enough glazier, in his mind, that he'd be able to suture up his window frame, with new glass, nice and easy. But for the time being, he had to get to the other side of that fence. And so out he tumbled, pausing to rest and repair aspects of his form in the street, so that no glass, nor debris, was upon him, as he preferred to greet whatever was on the other side of the fence as he would a date.

He was wise to adopt that attitude. The bushes on the side of his neighbor's yard provided excellent cover, and he trampled several birds nests as he went. The fence almost glowed, he thought, like a fire does in autumn, when the sky is darker, more purple than it is in summer, and the flames suck up all the light that surrounds them, like they need it to live.

He leapt around the edge of the fence with an attitude of "Aha!" as he hit the other side. He noticed the pubic mound first. Bushy. The skin was alabaster. She looked like her. She looked like the neighbor's wife, too. He knew, instantly, that she was resting, and was not to be disturbed. An attempt to do so, on his part, would have been, to the therapist's manner of speaking, backsliding. She was soft. That he could easily tell. Her legs pressed together, and curled towards her torso, arm under her head. The grass was matted down, in a shape similar to the pose she now struck, in several places. Upon returning the next night—or what he felt was the next night—she had been moved. So that's what they were doing. No sense killing the grass. It was very green. He'd go away and come back, go away and come back, over and over again. His focus, as always, was matchless, such that he couldn't remember where he went away to when he wasn't behind the fence. There was not a moment, in his mind, away from her.

She became less soft, over time. This was useful, though. Or practical, anyway. It simplified the matter of transport, and as he watched from his window, behind his new pane of glass, he saw how it was becoming easier for his neighbors to take her out into the yard, and soon there was no need for the cedar fence at all. Mr. P. himself removed it with a sledgehammer. One could hire him on—if you wanted to risk it—for an odd job or two. The marbleized form had lost what hair it had, but he could tell that was her, all the same, as she sat in the front yard, or the side garden, and the birds, no longer put off, provided easeful company, as his salt crystals--who, as it turns out, were not talking in code—now provided him with one new constellation after another.

Beyond the Brambles

Screaming Woods had crows, and Lorchen Grove had ravens, but apart from having their own resident species of ominous black birds, they had little in common, unless one wanted to count their rivalry, and the brambles that hemmed the edges of both.

The crows and the ravens were certainly aware of this rivalry. So much so that a crow, however bold, or however desperate for the sight of new vistas, or new dead things to eat, would not venture to Lorchen Grove for anything, just as the ravens were similarly steadfast. Some snakes, over time, had attempted to shift allegiances, but that's how snakes were, and probably always will be, so neither the woods nor the grove wasted any thoughts on their ilk.

Screaming Woods had an advantage, of sorts, in having existed longer, and traveled further. It dominated the countryside, with its blackened trees, and walls of nettles, which were also black, save for the feathers they had removed from passing birds who had gotten too close, some of whom had even been impaled, which caused the woods to laugh its deepest, most resonant laughter, with the aid of the winter wind that always blew through it, no matter if it was spring or summer.

If you passed through the woods, you were certain to hear that wind, although, weirdly, it was rarely felt. But if you heard it enough, you'd surely liken it to someone screaming. And if you heard it more than that, you heard a million voices screaming, or what you thought must have been at least a million. And they came at you from all directions, until it seemed there could be no more directions from whence they could come. But you'd find your chest starting to rumble, and you'd realize that they were coming out of you, too.

If you were bold, you'd ask yourself, later, at the closest tavern, where no one else ever seemed to be, but you and the publican, how they had ever got there. Was there something loathsome in you, that you were heretofore unaware of, in cahoots with the malingering spirits of those desolate woods? Were you like the woods? Had you made the wrong decision going into your trade, rather than, say, becoming a woodsman, or a gamesman? Since the way back home was through the woods, there was no way you'd be taking on even a corner of it again on that night, so you'd resolve to drink more than anyone should, and pass out in an alley, to make your way back in the morning, when the woods seemed more manageable.

This was a most impressive display of macabre-based virtuosity, and Screaming Woods knew it. Just as Lorchen Grove did. Lorchen Grove didn't have nearly the career, in terms of duration, that its rival had. It was but a couple hundred years old, choked with pines though it was. They gave the grove a greener aspect, but it was a blotted, blighty green, like the trees had become sick, or else dunked themselves down the chimneys of one of the neighboring villages, when no one was looking. That was one local legend, which was more workable, maybe, than most local legends, in those parts, because the boughs of the pines were indeed caked with ash, and if you grabbed hold of a branch, and gave it a pull, black clumps would rain down on you, stinging your eyes. And the moment you reached to them to try and rub that burn away, the boughs would gather on all sides of you, or so it felt, and it's not like you could see as well as you'd been able to under normal circumstances.

But the grove was not overly large, and if you ran, and it was not too late, you'd likely make it out into the clearing again, where the road was, after only falling three or four times. For the grove hid its nettles on its floor, and they were believed to have been tied in knots for the expressed purpose of snagging you, and pulling you down into the earth, by some old fishermen from the village who had died at sea.

Why there were employed in this manner, no one knew. But it also meant no one had any occasion to look to the water anymore, for the shapes of men, dimly lit, straggling up the beach, returned home at last. For this had already occurred, apparently, with no one noticing, and, like the ravens, the men, or the forms of men, or whatever one wished to call them, were intensely loyal to Lorchen Grove, even if Screaming Woods had tried to entice them by casting the rotted husks of some of its fish out into the clearing, where the road was, knowing full well that dimly lit men preferred riper flesh. Alas, in this matter, the luck was not on the side of Screaming Woods, and this caused further bitterness, and a blow for the upstart. Screaming Woods would have to redouble its efforts.

•

Neither rival knew, for certain, what would happen when a train track was laid in Screaming Woods. It was at the eastern fringe, which is to say, on the side facing

Lorchen Grove, and only crossed a fraction of the older forest. Still, Lorchen Grove anticipated problems. As did the glowing fishermen who hovered in its roots and brambles, and often took the form of a low-lying fog, so that no one could guess their number.

There was only one figure anyone ever spied on its own, and that was the form of the highwayman whom had given the grove its name. For he was a lurker, which, in his time, was known as a lorcher, and a most spicy Irishman who spoke in couplets and bursts of poetry, as he clambered out from behind the grove's many boulders, gun in one hand, and a knife in the other.

It was said that the nettles on the floor of the grove were red because of all the blood he had let loose from throats, and that no amount of rain, or washing up by the lower classes of glowing seamen, could drain away any of that coppery crimson. The glowing seamen were never spotted in the same place, at the same time, as the Irish highwayman. You might not know him to be an Irish highwayman, and if you saw him only once, you surely would have mistaken him for a thin column of fog, with a tapered top end. The fog moved—as if by a current—in radiating waves, from the tapered top down to the floor of the forest. If he was seeing you for the first time, he'd only show himself. But if you came across him again, he'd advance, as the leaves fluttered, despite there being no wind, with their ruffling producing a sing-song effect, like they were incanting some strange, marmoreal verse, the sort one would find on the outside of a crypt, which was fitting, as the Irish highwayman also spent a goodly amount of time in graveyards—when he was more than a column of fog, or less, depending upon one's views on these matters—composing his verse, and awaiting the next flower-toting widow to set upon.

Many of the widows made their visits on behalf of the seamen, and while one probably would have thought the seamen, in turn, would have their minds on revenge, in Lorchen Grove their energies were instead marshaled against anyone who might happen through, as was decreed by the spirit of the place. Besides: even the grove itself was frightened by the Irish highwayman. That he had determined the grove's name, and much of its identity, without the grove's input, gave him a certain dominion over the place, and so no complaints were made when mutilated ravens started turning up, with their flesh peeled back, like they were shucked ears of blackened corn, some of which were lobbed in the direction of Screaming Woods.

The latter wondered if this was a sign that its rival was, in some way, weakening, given that the Irish highwayman exerted so much influence. But it had been a while since Screaming Woods made a display of power, so it was difficult to gauge how its rival would respond, and how well. Granted, there were school girls who wandered in at night, that no one heard from again, and drunks, too. Always drunks. Many of the black thorn bushes that grew in great clumps in the woods were not black thorn bushes at all, but rather knots of centipedes, the lot of which had never made it into the record of local legends. But these centipedes were integral to the business of the place, for it was they who cleaned up all the flesh; which is to say, consumed it.

Lorchen Grove had no such system, and this was a weakness, doubtless, it well knew. For the grove did not have that same sense—not quite—of attendant mystery that Screaming Woods did, given that the bodies in it were always found, and a causality of death thought up. Hypothermia, suicide, heart failure. Whereas, with Screaming Woods, no bodies were ever discovered, and there were only so many times one could opine that the smithy had lit out for a better smithing job, somewhere, in the middle of the night, or that somebody's child had been snatched by fairies, because, in truth, everyone knew that there were no fairies in the area, given that fairies are airier, brighter things, and would not have cottoned to either oppressive wood.

There was, in following, no shortage of grim talk about the two spots in the taverns. Tall tales abounded, but they all came down to the same issue: which place was more unholy? It was a matter of local pride that two such spots existed within a few hundred yards of everyone's door. Arguments centered on how many relatives one had lost and where, or, more efficaciously, rants, theories, narratives, treatises on the spirit, the mood, engendered by each place, upon entering either of them. At some point you had to, in all likelihood. Screaming Woods led to a road that led into the city, where the courts were, and the hospital, while Lorchen Grove fronted a stream that teemed with fish, and had water that was said to have palliative powers, and, indeed, this was true, although no one could explain it.

Neither Screaming Woods nor Lorchen Grove was enthused to have inspired civic pride, for that was not their business or intention. Soon, it mattered little which was the more unholy place. In fact, the people of the town preferred to think of them as more or less equal, because lots of town had one unholy forest, in those days, but how many had two? Screaming Woods urged its winter wind on, and more birds were lashed to brambles, and the centipedes consumed and consumed and consumed, while Lorchen Grove, meanwhile, rained down more soot, and implored the glowing fishermen to build more knots, so that no one could take a single step without becoming snagged, and falling over, and having to crawl back to the road, as if in a posture of asking for mercy.

Sensing the need for reinforcements, Screaming Woods tossed out more hunks of rotted fish than ever, trying to tempt the glowing fishermen, but they had not been seen in some time, as the Irish highwayman was involved in lengthy, delicate talks with the spirit of Lorchen Grove, which lived inside the rock that was said to mark the Irish highwayman's intended resting place, though he had, of course, flown from it.

Both were quite concerned about the possibilities presented by the railroad. Screaming Woods was crafty; doubtless, it'd find a way to capitalize on the opportunity. The grove could become obsolete, and the grove that became obsolete today was tomorrow's arbor, with apple trees, happy children, and sunlight, which was a bane, most of all, for the plume of fog that was the Irish highwayman. The latter swore a most unholy of oaths to do what he could, and not worry so much about his individualism—for he always had a pronounced streak in that matter—and work with the glowing fishermen, if need be, to ensure as much evil as possible.

One suicide after another occurred in Screaming Woods, from the very first day that the railroad ran through a section of it. The woods were very influential; they had a way of seeping into a person's mood. The centipedes had been ordered to let the bodies lie, on the tracks, or near to them. The winter wind quieted down, so as not to prove distracting, whenever someone hid behind a bush, waiting to step out in front of the approaching car. No other suicides were reported anywhere else along the line, earning Screaming Woods further notoriety, to the chagrin of Lorchen Grove.

Eventually though, the conductors had no more fears that anyone would step in front of their cars, for a deal had been reached, after many long years of negotiations. The Irish highwayman was smarter than anyone had supposed. Screaming Woods, and all its parts, were shocked, one night, while pondering future unholiness, to see that thin plume of fog advancing across the clearing, riding atop a bed of glowing, vapory whiteness, which, of course, were the knot-tying fishermen. Shucked ravens were offered as gifts to the thorn-centipedes, who had been hungry for so long, thanks to the change in policy, regarding bodies, because of the railway developments. Upon the next day, and for many more, Screaming Woods and Lorchen Grove were quiet. It was said that each had a peaceful feeling about them, though it wasn't a peace that you trusted, not entirely, anyway, no matter how many uneventful strolls you'd had in either place, in the intervening years.

When the spirits of all involved had got to the bottom of the stream which had once had palliative qualities, the wisdom of the venture was undeniable. It was agreed that the rivalry, which would probably be a friendlier one, could be resumed in future years, when no one would be expecting it, back in the familiar haunts, which were now fallow, after a fashion. Meanwhile, the

Irish highwayman—who was more like a faint, rippling glimmer in the water—was saluted with the darkest, and most unholy of oaths. They'd have an easy time getting into everyone, now.

Secondary Drowning

He knew, naturally, that eyes could no more call out than an ear could issue a friendly wave, or a hand break into baritone voice. But he thought the eyes spoke, all the same. They weren't always there. When they were, it was typically a good sign. Sometimes he'd feel an elbow in his side, as though he'd been looking in the wrong place, and needed guidance.

The skunks would be back in the recess below the steps. He had never had a bad encounter with them. Not that he regarded them as brethren, exactly. The raccoons were even more to his liking, and they could be anywhere. Like him. Or almost like him. "Ours is a curious art. No rules. Strictly speaking. And yet, dictums. And decisions. Of timing. Strategy. Even artistry. I wish we didn't always have to wear these dark clothes though. It's enough to make you feel dreary."

He would sometimes feel the elbow again, but only if there was a rare and honored guest amongst them, and it was time for him to shut his mouth. A fox would do it. Or else a noise from up the stairs, on the inside. He'd been bit once. The fox ran off, taking his unblinking eyes with him. They rarely closed the garage door all the way, should there be occasion to tuck and roll, whilst flee-ing. They practiced several times a month on the foot-ball pitch behind the high school of whatever town they were in. When he came up chestwards, he'd look at the stars, and decide that they were steadfast fans, the sort who'd hate to miss a match, such as this was one, and who preferred—possibly because of their individual depths of passion—to sit at some distance from each other.

"I wonder if a tetanus shot will do. I'd hate for the full rabies course." The doctor asked him how he had come by his injury, and he told him that he was a hunter up in a stand, and the stand had fallen, and he had been knocked out, and something or other must have thought him dead. "Well, it's not a fox then. Fox don't eat carrion. And you're not carrion, are you?" The doctor had a stuffed striped bass over his desk. His eyes weren't real eyes, but he thought they called out all the same. When the doctor stepped out, he flipped the switch and pulled his flashlight from his pocket to see what he could. It was like being on a dock at twilight, inspecting the nets and patching the dinghy, and he spat on the striper. "That's all I have handy at the moment, mate. It's dry in here, isn't?"

•

He didn't think it was possible to enter a wall. He knew how to pass through them, when doors were not available. But entering one was different. The bed was like an atoll. It stood before him, as he bobbed along at its southern edge. He felt his side to see if he could remember the last time the elbow had been there, but the elbow was gone, and its owner with it. There was nausea, and he was ashamed that a man of his background should suffer from it, but he'd not been cast quite so adrift in a while, and he understood that it might take some time to get his sea legs under him.

He attributed his last bout of vomiting to the shots from the doctor, and not the celebratory tipple that they had drunk in honor of his surviving the fox, and their latest sale. Jewelry—more of the same. The going rate. But a dirty, dusty painting of whitecaps, now turned gray, and a half-masted schooner—a variety of canvas one associates with junk shops in coastal towns—meant the cash windfall of a career, to date, after matters of provenance had been established. The sea green wall beckoned. It swirled in pleasing ripples around the sides of the atoll, and he expected someone like his father to come wading towards him, eels in hand, a knife bulging out of the pocket of his lime-colored slicker, before decamping to a small room that would be filled with the smell of warm blood, displaced eyes, and heads that fluttered and nodded after they'd left their bodies behind.

"They're trying to swim away, aren't they boy?" He giggled the first few times his father made what became his regular joke, but over time he began to think that maybe he could ease the journey of these eels, so he put a bucket of cold sea water—the darkest, most clouded he could find without falling off the quay—at the end of the cleaning table, and placed each head in what he assumed would be considered a portal to freedom, and back to a more natural environment, a last comfort before life was left behind for good, and each head floated to the top of a most grim bucket.

"There's soup, son. Your mother's not going to mind that." The water was drawing closer, and it felt heavy on his chest, and the atoll began to fade into the distance. He suspected that the currents were not the kind that he should try and navigate. But he had always been a good swimmer, so he decided he would be better off moving deeper, where there would be no undertow to contend with, until he reached what he thought would be like a spigot, from which he would exit and gain *terra firma* once again, with reason for another celebration, although this would probably be one he'd undertake on his own, or with the owner of an elbow he'd not experienced before.

He pinched his nose, and with his free hand pushing him downwards, passed over the exposed blocks of coral that were stacked like steps. It took a moment for his eyes to adjust to the heightened salinity, and he thought it odd that only his free hand felt wet, and the rest of him entirely dry, save for the sweat that leaked out around his collarbone. He did not like to be leaving before his father arrived—even though he wasn't certain the old man would show or how many eels he would have—any more than he liked to think that this diving situation of his arose from anything more than an accident. "Help could well be on the way," he thought. "Let us hope it's not the Coast Guard again. Although maybe I shouldn't be picky."

•

He didn't think it was possible to enter a wound. Generally, he liked wounds, and all manner of gashes, serrations, and holes. Especially the variety that did not heal, because it was then that specialists would be brought in, individuals who saw an opening in a person and thought it a challenge, something to close up, for good, if not smooth over. There was something sculptural about that, and as they did a tidy bit of business in statuary antiquities, the concept was one he empathized with, and had occasion to try, from time to time, when their escapes had not gone so well as either of them had hoped—or as he, sometimes, had prayed.

He wondered if he should be doing so now, but then remembered the ribbons he had won in swimming contests at a summer fair, in a pond that had, for some reason, been pumped full of chlorine. He steered past the limp, floating forms of trout, eels, carp, dace, and was especially mindful of the pike, who apparently took a greater dose to kill, and who wished to exact some flesh of their own before they, too, turned up their white undersides to the sun.

There was a twinkling from high above, and he concluded that it must have been the fading rays of the sun, which barely touched the walls of water around him. The sun reminded him of a chandelier, and even at this depth the resemblance was uncanny, as the last vestiges of light danced upon the walls of water around him. The warm, sea green of the bay around the atoll was but a memory now. At each level the walls grew darker. Given that his line of work sometimes required a certain knowledge of paint and paintings, he was well-versed in shades. Surf green, grays harbor, lagoon, poseidon, raging sea. And then—brown. Worm-eaten brown. There was a hole in one of the walls, or more like an entrance way. He wondered if microbes viewed holes in the body as a diving tank, and whether they entered willingly, as though they had found, at last, what they had been looking for, or by accident, and just fell in, and had to look for a spigot of their own.

The nausea increased, which he attributed to the increasing pressure as he swam deeper. He thought it worthwhile to try and calm himself by using the water as a magnifying glass. Things that had been dim and far away came into view, and off in the distance he was able to make out what he determined was a wreck perched on a coral reef, with the seemingly endless depths of the ocean on all sides. He saw silverware, a galley stove, a sturdy oak table, a fireplace, and a hole in his side that did not sting, even though he was able to put his index finger all the way into it, and move it up and down.

He sent bubbles coursing upwards as he turned all about, making certain that the fox had not managed to swim up beside him. It was a relief to enter the strange vessel, even though it had a modern washer and dryer, which he did not associate with sunken ships. There were no fish anywhere, let alone one who might, as he had hoped, be interested in acting as a guide. He admitted that this was probably outside the line of work of most fish anyhow, save, perhaps, a dolphin, but dolphins didn't swim nearly so deep, and he knew they were mammals besides.

•

He made a desultory exploration of his new surroundings, but it occurred to him before too long that Neptune, or whoever happened to oversee these things, was probably a crafty fellow, and would not hide a spigot that would take him to *terra firma* in so ordinary a place as to feature a washer and dryer. He did hear a churning sound beneath him though, like water was being released onto something that was not water. The noise came from behind a door, which he presumed led to the belly of the wreck. He wondered if there might be a hole for things to flow through, and which he could flow out of too. Maybe that was where the owner of the elbow had gone, and taken his blade with him, because he was off in search of help, and thought it best to be armed for the simple reason that he did not know what manner of creature he might come across.

He did not understand why he remembered a punch-up between friends, although he knew that his father had been no stranger to such tussles, outside of the pub, after he'd been celebrating a particularly good catch. He was tired, and it was hard to think, and it was even hard to recall the name of the owner of the elbow, or his own name, for that matter, but he expected that the spigot would be a restorative, somehow, if only he could reach it, or find—for he still held out hope—a friendly fish to guide him on his way. He liked how his father would call him buddy or pal when they cleaned the eels, because he never called him either at any other time, and when he laid the heads of the eels into the bucket of the darkest, coldest water he could find, without falling off the quay, he would call each of them buddy or pal as well, and now he began to think that he had been their version of a guide to what maybe they thought was a spigot, and not his mother's steel soup container.

He pulled open the door that he assumed led down to the bottom of the wreck, and fumbled his way over the coral steps. This was the darkest level yet. The walls of water were a blackened hue of purple, and he thought of eggplants and wondered if there was an aquatic variety, as was the case with cucumbers. The surface of the bottom was cold and rusticated, almost like poured concrete that had not been distributed evenly. The sound was louder in his ears now, and then he saw a shape off in the murk. It looked like a basin of some kind, but surely his eyes were deceiving him. But here, at least, were other forms of life, though what a strange garden of life this was. He made out the floating head of a deer, with impressive antlers, coming out of one of the walls of water, and an enormous pheasant, who stood at attention in the vicinity of the shape that looked like a basin.

He thought about calling out, but he did not know what they could do for him, given that they were probably as far removed from their regular element as he was. Maybe they were hostile. One never knew. He looked around for the fox. He knew he could not go much further, and was about to stop trying altogether, and see what happened if he curled up and waited—he did not know for what—when, finally, fortune smiled upon him.

There he was after all: the striped bass, as good a guide, he thought, as one might wish for. He hoped he would remember his earlier kindness, when it had been very dry and he had provided what comfort he could. But he saw that the bass's eyes had gone missing, and deep, empty sockets peered back at him. He spat in the direction of the fish as a friendly reminder of their history, but the gob seemed to fall on his hand. He looked down to confirm this, and saw that the gob had turned into a running river of red, and that it was engulfing him. A beam of light appeared behind the striped bass, and he managed to push his way through a mass of kelp that felt like a thick curtain. He had come to the object shaped like a basin—with, blissfully, a spigot atop it. He couldn't tell if the water was emptying out or staying pat, but he figured this must be the exit, so he hurled himself in its direction, and penetrated a clear pane of water that shattered instantly, as if a magician had wielded some influence. The air filled his lungs and caused him to vomit, but as he rested his head on the cool clay—which, he perceived, was beneath a deck—he was certain he could make out the smell of eel heads that he had so long ago tossed into a bucket. He muttered back in the direction of the striped bass that he was a loyal friend, after all, and let one of his eyes fall shut, while fighting to keep the other open, in case the fox was nearby.

Dark March

There was no collectible Doze valued like his fully-assembled Aurora Dracula model. He was sure there was no other collectible like it, anywhere, even if it really wasn't a collectible, strictly speaking, at all.

He had never brought it to a toy fair, or any kind of fair, flea market, or swap meet, lest people start to talk, and wonder how Doze had come by such a rare and perfectly maintained find. Someone, surely, would attempt to put a dollar value on his fully-assembled Aurora Dracula model, and if Doze knew the model like he thought he did, problems could well arise, in the future, if one attempted to bring commerce into the equation.

His grandfather had given him the model kit, he was fairly certain. Bela Lugosi's face was on the top of the box. Doze had seen Lugosi play Dracula, many times, on TV. His father, he seemed to recollect, had laughed at some of the stilted dialogue, and he laughed too, pleased that they could be sharing a moment like that together.

But Doze was not a good artist, and after reading the instructions on the side of the model kit, he figured it was probably best to leave the assembling of the various parts, and the painting of them, to others. Maybe a friend could help. He wondered. It seemed wrong to try and jam everything together, slapdash, and end up with a creature who looked nothing like the one on the outside of the box. The monster on the outside of the box was one you'd want to look like on Halloween, only you'd have a hard time topping it the next year, and people would expect you to try.

But then Doze's grandfather drifted off, one night. Right past Doze's window. That's what he told himself, the next day. He believed it, too. So that when he later saw his father passing by his window, he knew to get up from his bed, and wave. His dad was stuck to the glass though, and that seemed wrong, because his legs, and his torso, clearly wanted to continue to drift in whatever current he was in, and it was only his hands, which clung to the sill, that felt differently. Doze's wave seemed to help matters though, because his father waved back, and once he did that, he was free to drift on his way again, continuing to wave until Doze could no longer make him out against the purple and black of the evening sky.

With all of the people floating past his window, in an endless march of bodies and faces, it seemed like maybe it was not unwise to get to work on the model kit, after all. Doze thought it was unhealthy to waste every evening just sitting and waving, and his wrists were starting to hurt, besides. Some faces in the stream of people who went floating past his window looked more familiar than others, but, then again, there had been lots of times he'd mistaken someone for someone else, and he didn't like the feeling of embarrassment when he was informed how mistaken he was. So he just waved to everyone. But eventually, he forced himself to pull down the shade, and get to work on his model kit.

He was dumbfounded when he removed the top of the box. He saw nothing but waxy, yellow pieces of plastic, in various sizes, and he had no idea how anyone could fashion anything like the creature on the top of the box. But he found that the work went quickly, and that he even had a knack for it. He had no need for the instructions, as it turned out, and just to show the world how confident he was—for Doze figured the world was always watching you, in some capacity—he tore up the sheet of paper advising as to what was best, and swallowed it down, with some orange soda that had been left to him by someone he didn't remember as well as he once did.

Fifteen minutes after beginning, he had completed his masterpiece. He considered how other boys had once made theirs. The inside of Dracula's cape was almost always red. But Doze, guided by his singular inspiration, had made the inside of the cape green. The face was not done in skin tones, or white, the two options which were generally favored, but rather in something akin to the ashen gray of a hornet's nest, or old logs piled in the woods when they're full of rain water and rot. Doze considered the color to be fittingly dust-like, as he was a big admirer of dust, and wondered, often, whether it came from bodies, or something more crumbly, like the piles of leaves he'd made in the past, in the backyard, so that he had places to hide away, and think.

Other times, long ago, he had sat inside the empty toy box at the foot of his bed. He'd pretend he was Bela Lugosi, lying there, for hours, believing that, eventually, someone, a Van Helsing type, would throw open the lid, expecting to find him asleep, and vulnerable. Only Doze was wide awake, and as alert as possible. He waited for his mother to discover him, but then he remembered how he had forgotten to wave to her, as she floated past his window, so it was probably unwise to expect her any time soon. He had waved to his wife, and that stopped her in mid-stream. She just hung there, in the air, like a glass figure in tracery. Her clothes didn't even ripple, and it was like the wind had stopped, even though Doze, previously, hadn't thought anything could stop that current, nor all the faces, and the bodies.

But by then he'd spent years with his favorite collectible, and maybe this was why it had always meant so much to him. He considered it more than a possession, like it was a part of himself, of who he was. He had known people who had their own versions of Aurora monster model kits. There was the Frankenstein creature, the Mummy, the Wolf Man. And lots of explosions. The monsters were lashed to cherry bombs, lit on fire, and tossed from bridges, ledges, roofs, chucked out of lives, willy-nilly, boom.

Doze liked the idea at first, so he got a cherry bomb, tied it to his Aurora Dracula model, lit the whole bundle, and threw it from his roof, which he had scrambled upon one night, to get a better view of the stream of faces that passed by his window. He wasn't sure how far back it went, or whether he'd be able to see its source. But from high atop the roof, he couldn't pick out any individual faces at all, and the stream looked more like a finger of fog that stretched from one edge of the lawn to the other, before getting lost in the cedars and sumacs, and the clouds above.

When he went to collect the remains of his Aurora Dracula model, in the morning, he felt guilty, like he had let it down, somehow. But there was nothing to be found in the grass. He was relieved when he found the figure, intact, on his nightstand, where, in truth, he expected it to be, because it did not seem to Doze like something that had so long become a part of him could be gotten rid of so easily. So he decided to place it in the empty toy box. The figure seemed like it deserved the toy box more than he had, back when he played at being a vampire, although it was not a proper coffin. In following, the Dracula figure would get out, from time to time, and Doze would retrieve it, always having to chase it down, as quickly as possible, so that questions would not be asked, for which Doze had no ready answers. Sometimes he found the figure by a stream, at a bus depot, a dinner table, in a car, at the bottom of a pool, and, more and more often, stuck to his wife's throat, or her heart, as she floated past his window, in the night.

He knew that his wife wanted no part of his fully-assembled Dracula Aurora model, but the figure had a way of imposing its will, despite Doze's own wishes. He would watch his wife attempt to send the vampire, in its green-lined cape, with its face the color of dust, hurtling towards the ground. Some nights, it was an epic battle. Other nights, the figure would give in, insofar as it had it in its nature to acquiesce, and Doze would come outside and collect him, and tuck him back away in his box, while he tried to come up with a practical resolution for everyone's issues with each other. Eventually he settled upon trying to saw the figure apart, and consuming its individual pieces, as he had once consumed the sheet of instructions. Maybe that would conclude his wife's ordeal, if he could just get the beast inside of himself, and then it wouldn't be like anything, at all, really, was lost.

He sawed for weeks, and used knives, too, and a lathe. The problem was that, eventually, he fell asleep, and by the time he woke up, the model was fully-assembled, again, having put itself back to the way it had been on that first day, when Doze closed the shade and got to work.

It took all of his remaining strength to will himself to remain awake until, finally, the pieces were small enough that he could get them down his throat. He fought the urge to retch, and throw them back up again, and even used his fingers to push them further and further down, toward his stomach. When they were all swallowed, he finally succumbed to exhaustion, and slept until it was evening again. Upon awaking, he went to the window, to see if his wife was floating more peacefully. But then he saw a new figure, first at her throat, and then at her heart. He wondered how he could be in his room, and in the current outside his window, at the same time, and braced himself for a trip towards the ground, unsure if anyone would come to collect him.

Incident at 7000 Hertz

He woke up feeling flabby around the edges, like he'd put on weight in the night, and turned a couple shades darker, too.

"Gonna be a bit of a tricky one," the voice opined, soundlessly, as was always the case when he wasn't being summoned into official duty.

"Maybe I can get me some residual coffee. That'd do the trick. Thin me out again."

The juices of the stomach—neighbors he tolerated more than he courted their favor—would generally claim most of the coffee, but occasionally there'd be a few specks of moisture on the wall of his sound studio, and the specks weren't so bad because specks of coffee were, as a rule, cooler than streams of coffee, and the voice liked to be in tip-top form, and not burnt, even when less-than-artistic tasks were required of him.

Everyone in his line of work understood that a lot of what you did, everyday, wasn't particularly glamorous, nothing that could make your name, or elevate you into the great canon of voices, which, naturally, was a goal of his, even if, as the years went by, he was coming to accept that his goal was more like a dream. Still, one got motivation where one could find it, and that was his. You could be a champion audiologist one moment, bewitching your fellow voices, as they sat in their sound studios, in silence, waiting for their chance—if they dared to take it—to compete with you, and not an hour later you'd be forced to turn down your volume, such that you were barely audible—which was like a death knell for a voice—and maybe stammer, and use more breath in your presentation than your actual, bona fide self. Or, as he had been made to do a lot lately, grunt.

Stammering was becoming a day in, day out norm for him. It was a drag. Especially because he thought he was nearing the apex of his art, or could have been nearing it, if only he had been "given his head." That was a phrase he'd been told to start using, after watching several horse races on television. He was commanded to use it a lot: at work (not his work, but the Moving Box's work, which is to say, his employer's work), the bars where the Moving Box sat and drank, on the phone (who was a peer of his whom he respected, even if he thought his art limited, although he never divulged this, of course), and several times in an alley, but the phrase was reworked somewhat there, in the presence of another Moving Box, a female one, and it was then that the grunting would commence, and he questioned whether he'd ever be afforded a proper artistic opportunity.

It was difficult balancing all of this with everything he'd been hearing ever since the MB had gotten his new job. They had a bigger television, and the MB must have decided that he wished to enjoy new forms of art of his own, so they'd sit there, with all of the voice's neighbors—the juices of the stomach, the nodes of Ranvier (who were as pompous as their name suggested), the irises (with their penchant for wandering and surface concerns), and the charming, and chummy, auditory nerve, who was his best mate, truth be told, even if they both regarded the other as a foil—listening to MBs—or their voices, rather—sing. The MBs on television were dressed in elaborate costumes, which pleased the irises, but what interested him most were those wonderful sounds, made in languages that were beyond the realm of his own programming, or his own training, anyway, but he thought he could go back to school, maybe. It was always a source of embarrassment that he had but the one mode of his own. But just as he was enjoying how adroitly one of his compatriots hit notes higher than any he could hit (he was more of an elocutionist, as the trade papers put it; that is, one whose sensibilities were more in keeping with poetry than music, although, as he sometimes noted, during the long business meetings which were like unofficial mid-day breaks for him, perhaps the gap between poetry and music wasn't so wide as he had once thought, and that made him enjoy the singing performances all the more) he'd be overwhelmed with the red juice.

Or he thought it was red juice, at first, anyway, because there used to be a lot of red juice, which was also sweet, for the bulk of the MB's life. But the latter was always making him say, "more wine, more wine, more wine," even when no other Moving Boxes were around. MBs tended to gulp the stuff down together, he learned from the television shows. He'd study the efforts of his non-singing contemporaries on the screen as well. Sometimes they really hammed it up. Left out their "r's," or cut the backs off of words and feathered them, as he thought of it, so that a word didn't end with the sound you got from letters—and how he loved letters—but rather more of the breath. When the voice inside the female MB with whom his principal lived started talking to him while he was watching TV, he'd almost lose it. Oh, goodness, could she grate. He wanted to shout back at her, "What kind of

artist are you? Don't you have any respect for our me-
dium? You're cutting those g's off of the words, and your
repetitions, frankly, are undignified. Why, some of those
sounds aren't even words! They could get a duck to do
most of what you do. A duck. And it'd be beneath him."

But he could no more make the remarks he wanted
than he could avoid putting into practice whatever the
MB demanded. That's how it worked. You knew that
when you signed on for the gig. He worried that the other
voice inside his employer's counterpart thought he was
a total loser, and maybe she'd find a way to get the word
out to everyone else. Maybe she had a way with being
influential. He'd heard about that. Everyone got the trade
papers. You couldn't help but get the trade papers. If you
so much as uttered a sound in the night, when the MB,
strictly speaking, was shut down, you got the trade papers; they flashed all over the walls of your sound studio,
and as soon as they flashed, well, you knew everything
they had to say. There was this massive exposé on some
voices who had developed voices of their own, and these
voices were sometimes audible voices, saying what they
wanted to say, rather than what they had been told. That
blew his mind.

"What? No way. Why, that's an oxymoron if I ever
heard one."

But he wondered. Maybe there was something to
those reports. After all, you couldn't just make up something in the trades, could you? Well, he supposed you
could. But it was highly unlikely that something that was
made up would make it all the way through the publi-
cation process, such that the nodes of Ranvier, irksome
though they were, beamed it into the walls of sound stu-

dios like his. Highly unlikely.

In time, he learned that the red juice was wine and that was what was making him feel bloated and heavy in the morning. For the first hour of every day, he was off his form. Clumsy, stumbling, rather than precise and nuanced. At his best, one of his chief skills was his ability to imbue a given word, or phrase, with multiple levels of meaning, like the real artists of his field did. It was true that you usually wanted just one meaning at a time, so that your peers didn't have to overexert themselves with the response that their MB ordered them to put in motion, but some situations were more complex than others. Like when his MB asked him to negotiate with the female MB with whom they lived. She was, he thought, not as nasty as his MB seemed to believe, judging by what he was ordered to say, and at what volumes. Oh, the things he said. New words that were never a part of his orders when the MB was at the meetings, at work. They were words reserved for the times when the wine entered into everything, and the voice knew that it was exceedingly difficult to make a word like "bitch" sound as poetic, as supple, as worthy of his trade, as, say, "insouciance."

But thankfully, he'd be tasked with longer words, and longer sentences, as more wine raced past him, in torrents, and he enjoyed the challenge of having to perform so well while becoming more and more tired, and trying to stay dry. He even relished the non-word sounds he'd make, as it became later in the evening. Sounds of pain, anguish, anger, guilt. These came out as powerful one syllable exhortations.

Sometimes, at night, as he read the trades, he thought he heard his counterpart trying to talk to him.

When they were in bed together, like this, it was rare that anyone used words. It was more a matter of sighs and moans, and snoring, which he hated, regarding it as the washing up portion of being a great artist, the behind-the-scenes dirty work that you were pleased no one else witnessed. But it did seem like words were coming from the other side of the bed, and that they were words meant for him, and not his MB, who was asleep. This was a violation of protocol, of course, but one that had only ever been drafted into the rules and regulations of their trade in case, by some miracle, there came a voice that had developed a voice of its own. The logistics were mind-blowing, as he well knew; for instance, would the voice have an artist of its own in a sound room, like he was in his sound room inside the MB? Maybe the wine was getting to him. He thought he had dodged most of it, as it came racing down the throat. The throat was a carpetbagger. He'd throw in with anyone. He remembered watching a show, late at night, with his MB, and the MBs on the screen took off their clothes, and piled on top of each other, two at a time. He didn't suppose he'd ever do a version of that with one of his fellow voices, but the act, and all of its spasmodic gyrations, interested him. On those nights, on the couch, the MB had him making sounds like the ones he made in the alley they sometimes went to, together, after a long day of meetings, and after a lot of wine at the bar. There'd be a female MB in that alley, but not the normal one, at home, with the bed, where his counterpart now was, still making those sounds. He knew he'd have to keep making those sounds, faster and faster, until the white juice appeared, even though, strictly speaking, the making of the white juice was not his department.

But he did learn the phrase "the town pump" from these evenings, and he thought the throat was akin to the town pump of his world, taking on all comers; there was very little it rejected. He would have preferred more decorum.

They made more and more appearances in the alley. As soon as this latest female MB got on her knees, he'd begin with his work, although it was not especially fulfilling. Precious little variety to it. His counterparts, in these situations, did not attempt to communicate, directly, to him. He was sure of it. Nor did he want anything to do with them, even if they had voices of their own, or if he did. He simply wanted to be done with the business of the moment as quickly as possible. Oddly, the site of the white juice, on the chests of those female MBs, made him hope that there'd be lots of wine that night. At first, he tried to get himself to believe that he wanted the challenge of dodging it, and performing at a high level, while impressing his counterpart in the requisite, late night back-and-forth with the female MB.

But soon he found that he absolutely needed that wine to perform at all, and he made no attempts to dodge the torrents that rained down the town pump. Then he would become louder than he had ever been before. He hadn't known he was capable of such volume. True, he knew that his MB wished for more control than he was presently exhibiting, but it was difficult to go louder than he had ever before, but not so loud that he overstepped what was asked of him. The wine did not help, but it made the evenings easier. For he was tired of the notes the irises were always sending him, about how wracked and tired the female MB looked, and how her own irises seemed distended, and her face always wet. She shook, they informed him. The gadflies.

He was relieved that the trips to the alley had come to an end. Or so it seemed. They had not been there in quite some time. Instead, it was night after night, in the bar. He got a good rest in the bar. Little was asked of him, save the "more wine, more wine," line. It wasn't always wine. He also learned the meanings of beer, gin, and whiskey. They stung his edges more, though, and it took longer for him to regain his form after a night of gin, say, versus a night of wine. On the gin nights, he'd be ordered to make noises that he'd never made previously. Some of them, he felt, sounded like walls of concrete being torn in two. He wasn't sure what the meaning of these sounds were supposed to be, but if notes were words, he felt certain that these words would not bode well for the person they were directed at. He asked the auditory nerve what he thought, and his conclusion echoed the voice's own.

After the longest gin night of all, he found himself unable to read the trades, beamed in from the nodes of Ranvier. It seemed darker than it had ever been. Something deep down in him ached, and throbbed, such that he wondered if he'd ever feel right again. Or if it mattered. Maybe the experiments in sound that he was being made to attempt each night went too far. He didn't know. And then he heard it. From several feet away. His counterpart. Yes, she was definitely using words. There was a variety of words, like babble, that were commonly produced in these situations when both MBs were asleep. But this was just one word, and not the babble. The same word, over and over again. *Help help help help.*

The next day, the MB did not go to work. They went to a shop. There were no alleys around the shop, so there'd be no white juice in one of them, and the voice was relieved not to have to return to grunting again. He did as the MB asked, and saw the result of his work: some manner of implement, with a tubular barrel, and a thicker part that fit in the hand. He recognized the device from some of the louder movies he and the MB watched together, when red juice would leak out of heads and torsos. The irises could barely stand those movies.

His orders were explicit, upon returning home: he was—and this was more important than ever—to not make a sound. Furthermore, he was to issue commands to everyone else, from the irises to the throat to the stomach on down to be as quiet as possible. Like he had any control over everyone else. Still, he did as he was told, even as he remembered that confusing word he had heard, a thousand times, the night before, from his counterpart.

When the word came out of him, he knew he'd gone louder than he ever had before. Past the 7000 Hertz threshold. It was unheard of. He didn't know he had it in him. The irises passed word that the female MB was running, running faster than they had ever seen her go, as he continued to say the word, not knowing what it meant, going louder in volume each time. It was strange doing something on his own, but not knowing why. So it was true after all. He'd probably become a legend for future voices. Maybe he had started a revolution. He pondered that prospect for several minutes, before there was a sound even louder than the ones he had been making, much louder, a fraction of a second after the Nodes of Ranvier made the announcement that darkness was coming, and, indeed, everything went dark.

Foxing

The drive-way would be less brown, but it was a start. Actually, he didn't think it'd be brown at all, and that could add to the confusion, which was already considerable. Then there was the trespassing element. That was worrisome. But no matter what: the sidewalk portion of the drive-way was fair play. Even on non-open house days. Definitely fair play, he decided, after thinking on the matter for longer than he could remember.

He could stand on it, no problem. Anyone could. No trespassing.

"It's like an estuary," he thought. "Where two ecosystems come together. Part private property, part public property. I'll stand there, then. Stake it out."

The years in the town. The name eluded him, but that had been no great worry, for a time. Didn't really matter. And was probably recallable if it did, he figured. So he let it go. The memories therein, though. Another matter.

They were getting swallowed up, somewhat, only not quite as he hoped they would. There was less swallowing, which was his wish, and more enveloping. He didn't like that. Because then everything coexisted. Nothing was got rid of. Some things just became more obscured. But they didn't go away. How he had prayed.

"Somebody, please, empty me out. She's emptied out, yes? Doesn't have to remember, right? Or else we'd have encountered each other, again, by now. And she never could remember anything with any specificity.

So, whoever handles these matters, if you'd be so kind to make me stop remembering everything, that'd be brilliant. Dead brilliant."

The salt. That was a definite recollection. The salt would start it. The salt in the air. As it had been at the house, up on the roof, atop the panes of glass he stared at, during the night, trying to determine if the darkness outside saw and observed him as he saw and observed it. Down at the shore. The beach. In the day and the dark. The sand, which was brown like the brown had been inside the home he was now searching for, trying to get himself to the open house. Or to see if there was one. There had to be, at some point, he thought, standing ankle deep in the waves, in his buff trousers, which blended with the sand.

Such a rare house. One that kept going down. Generations of basements, one might say, he joked, to himself, in the water, resolving to let it get up to his knees, so as to acclimate himself to the environment, best he could. How far the water came from. Maybe it came from another hemisphere. To this beach. Where it went into the sand, and died. To be followed by another wave of water, perhaps from somewhere equally far off. The succeeding generation. And the next and the next and the next. In the span of seconds.

Just like those generations of rusted-out browns that he cultivated in his basements, without knowing it, at first. He'd bring her down there with him. There was a chill. He liked it. She'd wrap herself up, and sometimes he'd wrap her up as well.

"Your sort doesn't work," he'd say. "Try my kind. You really must. You'll see. Easily the better way to go."

He'd drape her again and again. She came to expect the gesture. So much so that she stopped bringing wraps herself, for the evenings down in the basements. She never knew when he'd point out another level to her.

"See how the house keeps going down," he'd boast. "There's more below ground than above. And no one knows it but us. And you mustn't tell anyone. This stays here. In this, the latest basement. Or in the next basement. Once I discover it. Do you doubt that I will?"

She didn't. She had total faith in his ability to find one successive basement after another, just as she came to expect to see him outside, in the last few moments before the sun went up, with a ladder and a tape measure, attempting to gauge whether or not the house was growing shorter by the day because it was forcing itself down into the earth.

"I enjoy all of these basements, don't get me wrong," he said one night, as she stood shivering in the half-light. "It's not that cold. Relax. Here: let me get you a wrap." He'd flick his hands towards her, but no wrap came from them. But he seemed to think one had.

"Help me measure this latest basement, will you? I want to see if it corresponds to the height that came off the house last night. Oh, I know, you can't see it. No one can see it with the naked eye. You think our neighbors could detect something like that? When they're here every day? Maybe if they went away for a year and came back, they'd be able to tell. I don't look different to you, do I? And we've known each other how long? Of course, if one of us had left the other, however long ago, and then we had a reunion, here, in this latest basement, if we still had access to the house, you'd see that I looked very different. Do you understand what I'm saying? And why are you shivering so much? You're shaking the measuring tape."

Each of the succeeding basements was white. Seashell white. Like old clam shells that had never been scooped off a beach by a child and known the inside of a bucket. Or like the scallop shells he once encouraged her to gather, in a plastic sandwich bag.

"Go ahead. You can decorate outside with them. Make your mark on the house. See? I help you make your mark. Told you. I always will."

He made a kissing gesture, missing her cheek, which was a lot like the gesture he made later, with the wraps, in the basement. She dropped the shells by the back door mat. Some of them broke. He kicked the pieces aside.

"See? Nice. You did a good job. Told you you had an eye for décor. People would envy you your eye. No wonder you were the first to discover everything about the outside of the house."

He was proud that he was able to give her credit for that. Plus, it may have been true. He couldn't recall.

The basements became less white over time. He didn't notice it at first, but she did. She'd point at the walls, as if doing so would alert him to what was happening, in each successive basement.

"What?"

And she would point all the harder, making her arm stiff, and her face. It was only when she stopped pointing, after years of doing so, after the discovery of more basements—and subbasements, and sub-subbasements—that he realized what she had seen.

"Ah. Everything is going brown. Or is it red? Brownish-red. Rusty. Copper-y, you might say. Strange I've not noticed it before. I don't suppose it happened overnight. Still, that's a result of being down here every day, exploring. You'll remember the example I gave you about the two people who haven't seen each other in a long time, versus the two people who see each other every day. Are you cold? Here. Let me get you a wrap."

Before long, the only white either of them ever saw in the basements was when the house got shorter on the outside, and there was another level to find below ground. But the white wouldn't last long. It was like the inside of an apple, after you took a bite out of it, and forgot about it for a while.

He was the first to see patterns in the shades of brown. Sometimes old books had those brown patterns, he remembered.

"It's called foxing, in books," he told his wife, as she shivered. "Decreases the value. But it's cosmetic, more than anything. Doesn't actually eat away the page. That's what mold does. Why, once, I saw a pattern of foxing and it reminded me of these Indian carvings I'd found in the woods, as a boy. I thought that was dead clever of the author: like he'd embedded a secret message for an imaginative person to try and decode. I wish I had given the matter—both matters, actually—more attention. You really need to start taking Vitamin C or something. It's really not that cold down here. I promise you. Your teeth shouldn't be chattering."

The day he came to the final basement—and he knew it was the final basement because there was only so much house left above ground outside, and not a full basement's worth—the white went to brown almost instantly, the moment he turned on his light. He was very deep in the earth, at this point. He'd never had a need for a light before, but on that day, a light was paramount. For without it, he was certain he would not have been able to discern the shape of his wife, in brown, as she disappeared into the wall.

The house stopped growing into the earth. That was a comfort, at least. He measured every morning, before the sun came up, and then again just after it went down. The problem now was that the outside of the house, and the surrounding yard, was starting to darken in color, just like all of the basements had. And as the color got darker, his memories began to sharpen, and he wondered, for the first time, how he had ever become such an expert in wraps, or how he had ever acquired so many of them. He wondered if it was best to try and go into the walls himself, or if that would have been discourteous, since he had not been formally invited. So he left, and prayed that he could be turned upside down and emptied out, because, really, with whom could he discuss such a situation? Sure, there was ways he could put it. Incompatibility. Not enough respect of each other's space. One could always blame it on the kids one did not have, but meant to. There were examples of everything. Surely someone must have experienced something similar. But the second such a thought entered his head, he knew its folly, and how wishful his thinking had become.

So. The weeks of wandering. And then the months. Years. As far away from anything brown as he could get. Days in the sunshine. Walking. Or standing up to his neck in the water, in his clothes, thinking how clear it was, and how maybe if he stood there long enough, and hoped hard enough, the moment that he once believed was inevitable would arrive.

But there was no waking up, even if he still found that he'd pinch himself, on occasion, on one of his walks towards the sun. He didn't feel like he was getting any closer.

"Then again, I'm doing this every day. I'm me. Right here. Always in it. So maybe if I wasn't me, but I was watching someone like me, I'd say, 'damn, look how far he's made it since two weeks ago. Why, at this rate…' Could be something like that."

But he knew it wasn't. Anymore than he could empty himself out. There'd be an open house, at some point. He could get back in then. He wouldn't be barred. Anyone can go. And then he'd become the de facto tour guide, if he could get his nerve up, as he once had it up, in all of those basement moments.

"You think the kitchen is something, well, what until we go underground. How many basements do you have? One? And you? One? Get ready for something new then."

Only, he couldn't remember where the house was, exactly. For a time, that seemed like a mercy. But as he walked deeper out into the water every day, he found his own ignorance unnerving. He'd scour the clam shells on the beach for encoded answers, but with no luck. Until one afternoon when he took a deep breath of salt-laden air, and bent down to find a clam shell encrusted with streaks of brown, on the sidewalk portion of a driveway, a stray from a child's bucket. He picked it up and walked inside for the open house. The sign said that all were welcome. There was no realtor, though, no prospective buyers. He thought he saw a shadow of brown when he turned on the kitchen faucet, but assumed that was just another generation of water, the sort that lives and dies in the space of the taps being turned on for the first time in an age. He opened the door to the basement, turned both faucets on high, and went outside to resume his walk.

Fulmar

He had become so adroit at dropping clams and fish from the sky that there was talk—in the normal, chattering fashion—that some event should be organized, so that other birds, across a range of species, could compete with the fulmar, in contests of accuracy.

Whenever the men, in their various boats, were lost at sea, he was the first bird everyone, save the gulls, looked to. Granted, the men would have to be out there a long time, and the birds—who could be quite unbudgeable in these affairs—normally required some dramatic, prolonged display of suffering before they were moved to intervene.

Drawing lots did it often enough. The birds would gather in great clouds of feathers and beaks, trying to remain as undetectable as possible, despite their number, as the latest group of men, in the latest dingy, after many days, took a turn selecting splinters of wood, from a single man's hand, that were peeled from one of the seats. The splinters of wood would have been useful in building nests, as such finds were hard to come by at sea, but there was so much drama in the moment that this caused the birds no untoward grief.

The man with the shortest splinter would be shot in the head, and his fellows would consume him, as the birds themselves all knew the gulls would consume any one of them, if they happened to die, and a gull was the first bird to come along. As the gulls liked to explain, it was just something they did, and to not do it would make them less gull-like and, say, more plover-like. This was a winning rhetorical strategy, for there were few birds a sea bird respected less than a shore bird. They hardly even traveled.

"Pussies," one of the gulls would say, clinching the argument.

But it was difficult for the birds to remember, for any period of time, what they had just seen and heard, and sometimes, mere seconds after watching this strange ritual, they'd forget what had happened, or that there were any men in some kind of crisis at all. Then they'd look at each other, and wonder why so many species had gathered in the same place. The fulmar was less skilled when it came to forgetting. It's also why he thought the friends he hung out with were idiots. That couldn't be helped, though.

Sometimes they'd sidle up to him, when he was floating on a piece of driftwood, enjoying a nice meal of crab, or periwinkle with minnows—which was his favorite—and make a crass remark, in their ear-splitting way, like, "Say, fulmar. Why aren't there any others like you? I mean, what the fuck—you just some kind of rebel or something?" And because the other birds were so forgetful, the asker of this latest question would come along a couple hours later, and ask it again.

The fulmar tried to be consistent in his answers, but no matter how many times he labored to explain that his flock had opted to head south—because they heard there was better fishing there—and he wanted to remain in the north, the same petrel or grebe would become annoyed that the fulmar seemed so impatient and frustrated by having to answer a simple question. On some occasions, he'd up the level of drama in his answer, hoping, some-how, it would become more memorable, so he'd not have to say the same thing over and over again, every day.

"Look. We've been through this a million times. Stop. Stop staring at me like you have no clue what I'm talking about. Just trust me. Can you trust me? No? Fine. Never mind. Anyway, my flock went south. Better fish-ing. Yes, I know the fishing is lean here. That's my point. I want to stick around. Prove myself. Because, truth be told..."

By this point, the petrel or grebe who was looking on, listening, would start to get a little freaked out, like maybe the fulmar was more twisted, in his way, than the gulls were in theirs. Gulls were just something you ac-cepted. They loved their cannibalism. It was a tradition. A bird made allowances for tradition. But the fulmar—well, he wasn't supposed to creep you out like the gulls did, and it was worse that there was just the one of him. Gulls had a pattern of behavior. This guy was an enigma.

"Calm down, grebe. Sorry. Grebe #147. It's hard keeping all of you straight. Truth be told, I'm glad you've taken the time to reach out." When he came to this line, he liked to extend his left wing, in a gesture of gratitude. But the grebe would hop back a couple of inches, not sure if the fulmar was about to commence an attack.

"As I was saying...I feel I've been lacking. Yes, I've developed in skill with dropping the clams and the fish to the men we watch die, so that they can go on living—such as it is—a bit longer. And I'm proud to have stood up to the gulls—so many gulls—on that score. Because we all know what they want, don't we? But what do you know of nullity, grebe? Do you know nullity, as I do?"

The grebe would take off the moment the fulmar made the series of cries that signaled that word. And what a hideous series of cries they were, like someone had taken the most perturbed sound an osprey ever made and put several layers of electronic distortion on top of it, and then mixed in a garbage disposal. Eventually, no one called the fulmar the fulmar anymore, but rather Fulmar, as though he were not a bird, as they were birds, but something else, more like the men they sometimes saw, whom they'd note had their own labels of identification, before they forgot as much, only to relearn it later, for a time.

●

The men always came. Sometimes it took a while for them to do so, but eventually they would arrive. The first day, they looked frantic, like they had too much energy. The second day, less so. There was confusion, as though they had expected something to come to pass, which did not. By the third day, the terror set in. Fulmar knew it because of the eyes. All of those sets of eyes. They reminded him of the occasions he'd gotten a crab on its back, on a piece of driftwood. The creature would turn its eyes up at him, imploring for a respite, another chance to prove himself difficult to catch, knowing, all the while, that this is not how anything worked.

One stroke would do it. Beak on the center of the soft underside. The eyes would take one last look, and then they became less like eyes and more like berries, which he had on good authority that the shore birds enjoyed.

He'd float past the men, on his piece of driftwood. Sometimes they'd swat at him. The gulls loved that. They shrieked in the air, hopeful that this would be the day that Fulmar got his comeuppance. They thought him overly proud, with his strange cries, and his anti-cannibalism stance. There was talk that he was a shore bird in disguise.

"Why don't you head inland and find yourself a tree, Fulmar? A tree would probably suit a guy like you. Nice and easy life. Plenty of places to stand. But no, not you. You're too good to take the easy way out. Jackass."

He noted that while his fellow birds remained as forgetful as ever, in most matters, they remembered more and more about him, even though he was still put through the familiar rigors of answering questions he had already addressed.

When there were men who did not swat at him, as he floated on his piece of driftwood, he did his best to provide some comfort. And some sport, really, for the grebes and the petrels never tired of watching him soar high above the latest boat, with a couple fish in his beak, which he'd send hurtling towards the men. The fish would land in the dingy, and he would circle back underwater for additional morsels. Sometimes he'd land a small eel, or a couple sea cucumbers, and these, too, he'd send down from the sky. On several instances the men were unable to see him, due to the fog, or a passing cloud, and they got on their knees, and rejoiced, clearly having mistaken him for something else.

"What is up, Fulmar?"

"Please. Not today, grebe. Sorry. Grebe 147. It's been a taxing one."

"Saw you playing. Looked good out there. Hit the boat every time. Nice one. Had a big wager on you. Fifteen razor clams. With that new guy. Puffin 38. He's an idiot. So I'm like, 'watch my boy Fulmar over there, doing his thing in the air. Bet you fifteen razor clams he hits the boat every time. Not a single fucking miss. Boom boom boom.' So he thinks I'm boasting, right? Or that I'm out of my mind. One of the gulls lent me a tail feather. Stuck it on my head. Like I'm a badass warrior. And badass warriors are usually crazy. Of course. I mean, ever met a sane osprey? Exactly."

"Congratulations."

"Right back at you Fulmar. Keep up the good work. Always enjoy watching you throw. Or is it drop?"

"It's a combination of the two."

When the men could not see him, and got on their knees, he made sure not to reveal himself by dropping, and throwing, more fish, or crabs, after the fog had rolled on. He'd watch the men draw lots, and readied his ears for the gun shot. They never shot at him, or any of the other birds. The gulls were cowards, and hovered, laughing, far out of range. But the men who had gotten down on their knees seemed to have an easier time of it than the men who saw him, repeatedly, in the clear sky, offering up his latest catch. For he knew, as they did—just as all the crabs had, when he got them on their backs—that there was a natural end to these things, even if, strictly speaking, he could continue in his efforts for days on end.

But over time, he became more and more restless, and the nullity issue—that awful feeling of being useless, of having nothing worth living for inside him—worsened. He did not feel like he was proving anything to himself, really, and he worried that he had made a mistake in remaining in that particular portion of the sea, where he had once felt so certain he was meant to be, alone—at least so far as his kind went—and searching for a purpose that did not involve flight. Truth be told, he loathed flight, and drew a distinction between navigating the air, in one's particular environment, and taking to the wind and exchanging one environment for another, simply because it was easier to do so.

"Fulmar, please. For fuck's sake. You need to calm down, mate. Stop with that nullity noise thing of yours. Worst sound I've ever heard a bird make."

"Sorry Grebe. Grebe 147, I mean. Was I doing it again?"

"Yeah. You did it all night. You're doing it in your sleep now. Look: have a bit of razor clam"—the grebe leaned back, hacked a few times, and vomited up a blob of slime-coated mollusk—"and get your shit together. Are you going dropping, or throwing, today? To be honest, I'm not sure if I think it's worth my while to bet on you in your present condition. I could totally see you missing the boat."

"No. Not today. I'm going wandering for a bit."

"You're leaving?"

"Just for a while. I'll drift with the boat, get my head right, and then I think I'll explore. Not very far. You know how I feel about flight."

"How the hell should I know how you feel about flight?"

"I've told you like a million—never mind. Forget it."

"Consider it done. Better eat that razor clam before it freshens up in the breeze."

He floated with the men longer than he ever had before. He used his right foot like a paddle, and pushed himself, on his piece of driftwood, up to the dingy. The men had been floating for days. More days than most of the birds could count. Fifteen was about as high as anyone ever got, which is why a fifteen clam bet was a big deal. He had helped the men as much as he believed possible, but he did not like waiting for what he believed was the inevitable. No eyes scanned the horizon, anymore, for additional men, in larger boats. They never came to that particular area of the sea, and yet, all the men, in the small boats, seemed to end up drifting there. One of the gulls boasted that he had an "in" with the dominant current of that portion of the sea, but no one, really, believed him, given that currents were so elusive and enigmatic that they possessed a language that was thought to be undecodable.

"I'm a multi-linguist," the gull maintained, but even he knew that no one took him seriously.

That day, Fulmar left the men to themselves. Normally, he'd wait and witness the first gun shot. There would be another, later on. Sometimes, a man would refuse to do his part, and try to get himself under the boat, and down deeper into the water. This was an understandable position, from Fulmar's point of view, although he also understood how others could think it selfish. The gulls considered him a hypocrite, but as he pointed out on numerous times, a gull who happened upon a dead gull and decided to eat him was, in effect, making a culinary selection based more on tastes and preferences, than urgency and need.

"Well fucking naturally, Fulmar," the gulls would

cry in unison. "Gull tastes fucking delicious. And let's be honest—who doesn't get sick of the crabs and minnows and clams?"

Some arguments simply were not worth making.

He was away longer than he intended, but the moment he left that hardscrabble portion of the sea behind, he knew he'd be looking for something that would not be easy to find, even though he was certain it was out there. When he first came upon it, he knew, instantly, as though one of the currents had spoken to him, in a language as clear as his own, that this was what he must face, and it was here that he must come, as many times as necessary.

Quite a few of the birds did not recognize him upon his return.

"Look at this. We got a fulmar. When was the last time anyone saw a fulmar?"

But Grebe 147 had become better at remembering, and had also acted as a stand-in, of sorts, doing his best—after betting on himself—to drop clams, crabs, and minnows to the latest men who had arrived in the latest dingy.

They floated on a shared piece of driftwood deep into that first evening after the great discovery.

"You're sure then."

"Yes."

"Is it really your place?"

"I think it needs to be someone's. All things considered. Context and all."

"I wouldn't want to do it."

"Nor do I."

But he did it nonetheless, with a beak crammed full of food, all the food he could fit in it. At the first sight of the gun, after however many days that took, he would fly low over the latest dingy, revealing the bounty in his beak, and he would fly as hard as he could, and the dingy, and the men, would follow. It was said that he made some pact with the watchful current, but no one, naturally, could tell for certain whether he had learned to speak that flummoxing language, or how. As the dingy traveled over the sea, the men became strangely like many of the birds were, in matters of memory, and soon they had no recollection of the fulmar in front of them, leading them on to a vortex of water, with an opening as wide and long as the boat they were presently sat in.

No one ever again heard him shriek his horrible shriek in the night, or at any other time. It was believed, so far as anyone could remember, that men stopped coming to that portion of the sea. Only one bird was certain, and, in time, even Grebe 147 came to forget who he was.

"You looking to stay here, fulmar, or are you just passing through?"

"Just passing through, mate. I'm a big flyer."

"Good luck to you then."

"And good luck to you, too, sir."

The Bowsprit

For years, Captain Doze had been considered the most ruthless soul in all of the British navy, and yet he fretted that he did not possess the imagination to make a critical and financial windfall befitting his ruthlessness as other, less wicked captains had, despite being less wicked.

His ruthlessness, in and of itself, was impressive, and it did him credit that he was able to keep his pride in check, no matter the levels of reverence that came with his latest display of wrath. Like when some cowering midshipman, just into his teens, would literally defecate in front of him, after committing some minor offense—like not polishing the sextant to a sufficiently bright enough hue—and one of his lieutenants, his voice quaking, would say something along the lines of, "Captain Doze, your wrath is most estimable today, sir. Why, the lad has shit himself, and you did not even have to raise one finger. Nay, not one finger."

Other captains—for this was an era when rage and wrath were valued more than gold and rum—would delight in such praise, and more than a few would be so empowered by it that they would turn on the hapless, useless soul whom had offered it up. And then a finger would be raised. As would the stakes. The midshipman just barely into his teens would have some measure of revenge on the lieutenant who had sought the captain's favor at his expense, for now that lieutenant, a turncoat if there ever was one, would be executed in a new and novel fashion, the likes of which no imagination—or any imagination possessed by any member of the ship's company, any-way—could have conceived.

Captains like Crimeney, Jameswot, and Thallerson, oh were they ever ragers and wrathers, but they weren't nearly the rager or wrather that Doze was, but they possessed what the men of the admiralty called "artful aspects and humors." Which is to say, they were creative men, and they'd contrive means of punishment that were so poetic that they made Doze weep, both for the quality of that poetry—he likened it, as such a sensitive man of his times would, to the verse of Richard Lovelace, with maybe a soupcon of Sir John Suckling—and his own shortcomings.

He had heard the recent news: Jameswot had build a kind of trebuchet that hurtled a man downward into the deck like God had shot him out of a pistol at close range. He loathed the notion of envy, and thought it one of the most sinful of feelings (as he made a *nota bene* to himself: "Are feelings, in actual fact, potentially sinful, or are they emotional occurrences instead, and not, therefore, strictly controllable, or indicative of rectitude, or a lack thereof"), but how could he not be envious, when he learned—courtesy of one of Jameswot's typically baroque letters, with his customary verbosity and allusions to Hobbes and Heraclitus—of the myriad directions in which the innards went, and how many men, despite long careers at sea, had vomited, and not even had the time or self-possession to do so over the decks, thereby creating more subjects for more displays of art, were the captain of a mind?

And so Doze retreated to his quarters, and ordered his steward to fuck the fuck off, as he put it, to brood on a familiar, haunting subject: Why had the muses of wrath and rage cast him as someone whose rage and wrath surpassed anyone else's on the high seas, while not arming him with the requisite ingenuity to put that rage and wrath into action? How he longed to be influential.

For years, Captain Doze positively leaked bile from the quarterdeck of his beloved ship, *The Imbroglio*. Other captains, like Crimeney, the detested Jameswot (who had lately penned a stage play about an underwater kingdom, inhabited by long-deceased classicists, that was all the rage in London, after a trial run in Portsmouth), and Thallerson, on other ships, were notoriously put off by masturbation, but Doze enjoyed the sport himself, and loved his ship so much that when he came upon a man busying himself in the pursuit, he would—and this was the only activity that would engender such a reaction in the detail-oriented captain—advise the man, boy, or young boy, to "continue pumping away at the main splice," and to "coat the ship, frost it as one of a delicate nature, like the poets Lovelace, or Suckling, would frost a cake, had they not bitches to do it for them."

He'd stand watching, until the deed was complete, no matter how long it took, and, truth be told—although no one would dare say as much—it generally took much longer when Captain Doze was behind you, fingering his glass—with which he usually looked for other ships that he could attack, and birds, for he was a great admirer of all manner of seabirds—as you labored. And finish you must, lest you get keelhauled, meaning, tied to a rope fastened to the ship and tossed over the side, to be dragged along the bottom of the vessel, which was coated in barnacles, and apt to tear you up, or tear your head off, depending upon how much sail was presently in the masts, and how much wind was presently in the sails. Effective—as these things went—but boring, and artless, and Captain Doze came to loathe himself more and more for his lack of imagination, every time he had to turn to his old standby.

He resolved to try a laudanum course. Rum was well and good, but it did not inspire him as he had hoped, and after reading—in the latest missive from the accursed Jameswott (who had recently been made a peer, in large part because he had reinstated a policy of droit du seigneur—in which lords could deflower their vassals' brides-to-be—in several northern parish towns)—that Socrates came up with his brighter, more creative thoughts, under the effects of hemlock, he decided to become a laudanum addict, and await the desired results.

It took a few weeks, but there they were, one morning, as he ham-fistedly frosted his quarters—or the portion of the floor by his piss bucket, anyway—in a shaky daze. He could not see colors anymore, but this troubled him not, as colors had a way of complicating moral matters, as he heatedly declaimed to the vile Jameswott in a philosophical letter of his own which argued that there were not shades of gray, but rather only the colors black or white, which is to say, right or wrong. "Lest ye wish to be judged a relativist, you bounder. And what is a relativist but one who says there are no absolutes. And yet, what is that, but an absolute in and of itself?" It was good to vanquish Jameswott in such a fashion, even if he wished such victories were not confined solely to epistolary matters.

But as he pumped and he pumped and he pumped,

in anti-relativist black and white, and he caught sight of his whitest spurt to date, the idea came to him: his bowsprit, that tusky horn, that indefatigable lance at the bow of his ship, why, he could hang a man from it, in, say, a basket, and that man could hang there as his hand now hung from his own mizzenmast, and the man would not be treated to laudanum—as that was a captain's privilege—but, say, a pint of ale, and, for sport, he shall be given a knife, and a loaf of bread. He immediately gave orders to pull into the nearest port, where he had fliers on the subject printed for his men, and for the admiralty, so confident was he in this most artful of ideas.

He even walked his crew through the idea of the piece: there he went, out on the bowsprit, wobbly because of the laudanum, but no one wished for him to fall in, for it was apparent to all that *The Imbroglio* was on its way to being perhaps the most respected ship in the fleet, and not the butt of so many jokes, as it had been for so long, with its tired acts of keelhauling, while the likes of Crimeney, Jameswott, and Thallerson dazzled the readers of the *Naval Gazette* with their heroically inventive works. It was said that Jameswott was working on a piece that involved flash powder, iridium, and a glowing cat o'nine tails—plus some trained ship's rats, with filed teeth—that would be the doozies of doozies.

In fact, there was chatter about Jameswott—although it occurred to Captain Doze that he may have imagined it, for his mind, as he rightfully understood, had become awfully fecund, thanks to the laudanum, which he hoped someday to be a spokesman for—amongst the crew as their captain headed out to the wicker basket fastened to the bowsprit, pot of ale in hand, with bread and blade tucked under his arm pit.

"He omits the mental aspect, he is a grave omitter, that Jameswott. For there must be tension. Not mere pyrotechnics. Now watch."

And they did, as Doze departed into the wicker basket. Nothing happened, at first, and then they heard his voice, somewhat muffled, but clear all the same.

"Now, what I can do is—which is to say, what some of you will have the chance to do—is to take this here knife (I've pulled it out, and I'm waving it in the air) and cut through the basket, and boom, down I go—rather, down you go—into the water, to be run over by this beautiful ship of ours, which we've all frosted so many times, to show our fealty. That's one option. The other is to dine. Enjoy a loaf of bread, and a pot of ale, which has had lime squirted into it, so it won't spoil, if you want to delay gratification. But wait! The bread's been eaten, the ale's been drunk, can I have some more Captain Doze, no you can't, you fucker, it is dying time, do you want to starve, or get run over by the ship? Pick! See? Tension. Drama."

He was so pleased by his ingenuity that he had taken down his trousers, and considered the edgy element to what he was now contemplating, before deciding it would keep for another day since the crew would probably appreciate a second demonstration. New men were always being pressed, and his tutorial, he concluded, would make for a wonderful theatrical piece, and maybe, just maybe, he could have a London engagement of his own, and so he shouted, to the confusion of the men, "And here be my Portsmouth, here be my Portsmouth."

Within a matter of weeks, *The Imbroglio* was kitted out with members of the admiralty, members of the nobility, members of the wealthy classes, and maritime legends like Crimeney, Jameswott, and Thallerson, so that the latest sensation of the high seas could be observed in person. Wagers were made, scholars were called in, and a revolution in mathematics was set in motion, as one scholar tried to best another in crafting a theorem that would enable a person to know what, say, man number five would do, when his turn in the basket on the bowsprit came, after the previous four had gone, for example, run over-starve-run over-starve-run over, or if they'd all opted to starve, or whatever permeation of the two options had occurred.

"Well, you are redoubtable, sir, you are redoubtable. I grant you that."

Doze liked to imagine how the vile, and now bested, Jameswott would offer up his congratulations, but they never came. Jameswott looked on, and placed his wagers, and before long he had more money than any man in all of England, for he knew—he always knew—whether a man would pick starvation or getting run over. He bought up one manor after another, and soon he had the whole of the northern territories under his domain, with schools where youngsters—for when their time came—could be taught in the revived droit du seigneur ways of yore, with plans for making inroads in the south, in the near future.

Late at night, Doze would shamble over to the man who had the evening's watch, and relieve him of it, an unprecedented act for a captain, but he wanted his privacy, and to smell the clean salt air, a luxury not afforded to him by his cabin. He'd climb out on the bowsprit, and hunker down in the latest wicker basket that had replaced the one before that had gone down into the sea. It was not nearly so titillating as it had been, previously, with the ship's crew behind him, but it made for a quality meditation chamber. He ate the loaf of bread he had brought with him, and savored the ale. Had he made a fool of himself in applying for an instructor's post at one of Jameswott's schools? He knew he was not qualified. His head was spinning, so he poured laudanum atop it, and opened his mouth, so that his lips could collect what ran down his face.

"Well?"

"Well, obviously," Doze responded, back upon the firm footing of his ship.

"Was I right or was I right?"

He hated dealing with Jameswott like this, after having been in his basket only moments before.

"Yes, you were right. I picked neither. Clearly. How much did we wager again?"

"Forget it. For now. We'll let it ride. Until the next time. Or we can take it out of your pay."

"You mean…"

"Yes. We'll start for the north on the morrow. You're gonna love the shit we do up there."

Doze knuckled his forehead, watched his brother captain walk away, and returned to the inside of his basket. Safe inside again, he reached for his knife, and cut himself loose.

"What a moron," he thought, as he hit the water.

With the money made by Jameswott—from the king, no less—droit du seigneur, properly financed, became general over all the land, thanks to Captain Doze, a bit of information that, naturally, Jameswott always fought—and successfully, too—to suppress.

Fizzy Scotch

Long before he met the lawyer Zoed, and long before he became a film buff, Padraig understood himself to be a doomed Irish poet, albeit with certain caveats.

The first was that he was not doomed in the sense that his life could only work out one way, with an unseemly end. The second caveat had more to do with his idea of what a poet was: someone who talked in a given way, and, in turn, wrote in such a way that he could not be anything but a singular figure, a lone wolf amongst his fellow man, which was a certain kind of doom, in the grand social scale of things, albeit a romantic one.

Or so he liked to think as he dashed around the various cities where he and his partner—whom he thought of as almost his straight man—Lorcan went about their various crimes and scams, with a pencil nub behind his ear, and a Walgreen's notebook in his pocket, lest inspiration strike. As one whose avocation was verse writing, he tended to think in nobler terms, and tried to get the fair Lorcan to understand that they took crime to the level of art when they forged antiquities, or commissioned art forgeries that scholars came to puzzle over, asking themselves if the latest crate of canvases, magically discovered in a Nantucket farmhouse, were by Jackson Pollock during a transition period, or a Pollock acolyte.

There were loads of lawyers over the years, plus agents from INTERPOL, and the feds. Highly inconvenient. But there was no lawyer like the lawyer Zoed, who may or may not have been real, and then turned out to be exceedingly so, as far as Padraig was concerned. At first he wondered if that was because there was no one like his wife. Lorcan did not know what to make of the letter Padraig had first sent him, just before the Zoed business began.

"Fellow artist," Padraig had begun, in his tight handwriting, in words so small that at first glance they looked like code, "the bachelor days have surceased. I will not indulge the spirit of caprice that is attempting to prevail upon me and say that we are one, but we are something, she and I, as you and I shall always be. Until our next round of artistry, stay free, me boyo."

It was the first time in their career that Padraig and Lorcan were not together. All of the years of crime—or art-making, depending upon one's views—had earned each a vacation, of sorts, a chance to pursue solo enterprises, like the members of KISS had, as Padraig pointed out, in the late 1970s, to various degrees of success. As a doomed Irish poet, he couldn't help but be struck by the name of Molly, and he was pleased that his wife should have such a name, so he ripped out the pages containing Molly Bloom's soliloquy from *Ulysses* and read them aloud over and over again, until he no longer needed those pages to know all of the words that were upon them.

But he soon discovered that a name only goes so far. True, this first experiment in love had produced a real love, so far as he was concerned. It was not a logical love, given that it was founded upon small peculiarities, like the way his beloved seemed to glide, or float, when she walked, towards him, but not when she walked towards anyone or anything else. Then again, he wasn't sure how logical love ever was, even in the most traditional cases, but the very word *cases* alarmed him, as if the sounding of it in his mind bespoke of future problems, and future courthouses.

He began to note that his Molly was not nearly so voluble as the one in *Ulysses*. In fact, she never said anything at all to him, which was not an easy thing to deal with for such a loquacious man. Actually, she ignored him altogether. It was a dilemma every time he wondered whether or not to ask if they should stop the car for yet another beer, as drinking was a sport which Padraig was most fond of. He knew that asking the question once would mean he'd have to ask it five times before he got his answer. And when that answer came, if it ever came, it would be at such a low volume that a further two questions, at least, asking her what she had just said, would be required, and this was a huge outlay of effort, to say nothing of the toll that the frustration took on him.

Talking aloud and not getting any response back made him lonely, and Padraig did not like that feeling. Then again, it was so hard to resist another glass of Miller High Life, even if he had lectured Lorcan, on one of their earlier adventures, when they were hid out in a modern ghost town, near Bridgeport, Connecticut, that there was no way "this is the champagne of beers. And who the fuck wants a beer-champagne hybrid? What would possess someone to attempt a blend? You want beer, you want beer. Not champagne. Different kind of bubbles. Got to keep the libation races separate, so to speak." And with that, he'd chug down whatever stash of potent potables, as Alex Trebek put it—for both Padraig and Lorcan were big *Jeopardy!* fans—that they had managed to round up, and would pass out within the hour.

So even though, as a poet, and an artist-criminal, he understood the value of silence, he could not abide silence all the time, and when he wrote Lorcan, then stationed in Newcastle-upon-the-Tyne, for his counsel, his friend replied that maybe someone was attempting to gaslight him, like in that old Charles Boyer film. This was confusing. Padraig had never seen the movie *Gaslight*, but he resolved to get away from his Molly and her silence, and take the first of several trips to the local library, where he went into the video room, found a copy of the film in question, and chucked it out the window, walking around out back to the garden where the tape now lay, so he could take it home and study it.

"I do understand your concern, Lorcan," he wrote, in his tight hand. "Only, the male and female roles are reversed in my own situation. But yes, I believe she is trying to drive me mad. For our money? Maybe. But I think more for the piquancy of taking on a poet, and trying to destroy him, by inciting him to lash out at her. I suspect she wants to be the muse for my prison verse, once she has fulfilled her role in getting me thus incarcerated. Some of the best verse, as you know, thanks to my lessons on the subject, come from within prison walls. I shall monitor the situation carefully. A handshake in my thoughts, to you, dear sir."

But he did not prove to be an effective monitor. There were more questions than ever, from him, and he challenged himself, daily, to come up with a subject that would rouse her brain, and compel her to respond. But nothing worked.

"What would you say about buttered kippers for lunch? For a picnic lunch?"

"My, this New England weather of you Americans. Of you northeasterners. Is it always so quick to change?"

"What do you think about me going hole to hole to hole on you tonight? The two right next to each other, and then up to the mouth?"

Nothing. Just silence. Padraig didn't believe that anyone wanted you to hit them, but it was starting to seem that way, and he was so confused that he began to wonder if Molly really existed, or if he was simply imagining her, every day.

"Such is the fecundity of the poet's mind, Lorcan," he said in another desperate, late night letter, as he guzzled the High Life, feeling guilty, maybe, that perhaps it wouldn't be so bad to cut it with champagne after all.

"To get the fucking piss out," as he wrote. Which gave him another idea.

"How about we piss on each other, in the tub, bit different, spice things up, as you Americans say."

It wasn't that he was interested in urine. Just a response. But one was not forthcoming, nor was one ever forthcoming.

He became more and more concerned that his creativity had overwhelmed his conscious mind, and that he wasn't married at all, and that he had entered into some misty realm known only by vanguard poets, where it felt like you were alive, and walking around, and swatting the mosquitoes that bit you, but you were off somewhere else, somewhere far less corporal. So he began to yell.

She quaked as he yelled. So fear registered, at least. She began to shake whenever he started to open his mouth. Eventually, there was no more yelling. She was gone. The house, empty. He took a hammer and smashed it through the wall.

"So it is real. It's there. You can't put a hole in something you've made up."

He made another, just to be sure.

•

He kept watching the films he had liberated from the local library in the mostly empty house. He found a mattress outside in someone else's trash, and dragged it into what had been the master bedroom, where she had left him his TV.

"Probably so I can continue my filmic education," he thought.

Within a couple weeks, a summons appeared. He was to meet with a Mr. Zoed, esquire, of Cambridge, Massachusetts, a Harvard man. To discuss terms. So her proxy would use words. That was interesting. And confusing. He drank more of the High Life, and wrote Lorcan in between film screenings. And he slept on the mattress, on the floor, while listening to Robert Mitchum, in *Out of the Past*, one of the classic film noirs from the 1940s. He slept well to Mitchum's voice, as he imagined children would sleep well to some of his poems that featured the adventures of aquatic animals, like lampreys, hagfish, crabs, jelly fish, gulls, fulmars, and tiger sharks.

Padraig liked when he knew he was dreaming. He didn't always know. He had a pretty good idea that Lorcan would have enjoyed Robert Mitchum's performance. He had one of the best lines Padraig had ever heard, upon realizing that, as they say in those old film noirs, "the fix was in."

"So there he is, Lorcan. Totally fucked. He is the dumping ground for everyone's problems, everyone's issues, everyone's agendas, everyone's lack of having a full story, and dodgy motives. The cops, his boss, henchmen, a mute guy, his old girlfriend. It's a ritualistic sacrifice. And so he turns to the woman who's responsible for bringing all of that together, who works the various story lines, and, knowing he is fucked and there is nothing he can do about it, he says, "well build my gallows high, baby." As in, takes a tall gallows to hang a big man. How brilliant is that?"

Such an individual could have even joined them as a third partner in their artful schemes, if he actually existed in the real world. Maybe a version did. Padraig resolved to be watchful. And then he would pass out. When Padraig realized he was dreaming, he knew he had *carte blanche* to do what he pleased, and he didn't have to worry about lawyers or agents from INTERPOL.

Padraig gave way to Dream Padraig, as he dubbed this nocturnal character to Lorcan. "Or, as I sometimes term him, DP, which you should not, for a moment, understand to mean double penetration, a term I have lately learned as my cinematic interests keep ranging further afield. But my guy has a wonderful knack for coming upon a gun store, followed by a knife store, and a poison store, every evening, each hawking their wares in giant flashing neon signs. So in he goes, dear Lorc, my somnolent self, picks up all the weaponry you could ever want, and it's time for a killing spree. Doesn't have to be a spree. You can just do one person. And it's free. No risk, no penalty. You have to make sure it's a dream, of course. The stores are usually a good sign. But they're not always there. Sometimes he just finds the weapons on him. That's more risky. Because maybe it's out there, happening, and artists like us have to pick our spots, naturally, in matters of exchanging life with death."

He hoped that Dream Padraig would have occasion to visit, and disembowel, the lawyer Zoed. He was an ugly, evil man, and, thanks to his efforts in acquiring a cinematic education, Padraig immediately likened him to Jabba the Hutt, in human form, and before too long, the lawyer Zoed was turning up during the poet's days and nights. It became increasingly difficult to separate the two.

"Are you going to give us the info we want?" Zoed stammered, his fat finger punching the air at the end of each word, and coming within an inch of Padraig's chest. This was troublesome. Padraig preferred, of course, not to cause a man to swallow his tongue by beating him in the throat in a courthouse, but he also had a strong feeling that it would be highly unlikely that he'd be able to avoid such an outcome, if this ambulatory—but barely—Jabba figure made contact with him, as he was close to doing.

"I only live on a bit of floor, upstairs. By the telly. That's where my VCR is. And where Robert Mitchum and Charles Boyer are. So I'm not sure what information you could be referring to."

"The fuck you don't, you fucking maggot. You almost killed the bitch."

The terminology, and even the argument, seemed oxymoronic. Padraig wasn't sure what to say.

"Almost killed her of what? Did Dream Padraig do something I'm not aware of?"

Zoed stared at him like he was crazy, and Padraig had seen that stare enough in his career, and his travels with Lorcan, to realize it was time to reign it in.

"Or, rather, what did I nearly kill her of? AIDS? Renal failure? The bacteria that passes from ass to mouth—which is to say, when one goes ATM?"

"By volume. By screaming."

"You can't die by volume. Anymore than you can die by silence. Trust me. She tried to do me in, on that score. I think. Or maybe she wanted to be my prison muse."

He saw Zoed start to look frightened and alarmed again, more so than Padraig ordinarily made people look frightened and alarmed.

"Yes, well, Zoed, I will sign over the house, to my soon to be former wife. And be on my way."

"It's not that simple," the fat man stammered, again, jabbing the air with his finger.

And so it turned out not to be.

The days in court, the words she used then, all of a sudden, as Zoed smiled. Padraig worried that some of his past transgressions would get a fresh airing, and if this happened, it might be some time before he could rejoin Lorcan, as he was presently planning to.

He signed a lot of documents forfeiting funds, property, as Zoed looked on from across myriad tables, laughing. Molly did not laugh. She simply stared, hard, like she was looking into him so as to look past him, to whatever was beyond. He'd turn and look, but it was always the same wall, in the courthouse concourse, with an oil painting of a man wearing a wig upon it.

He decided to be romantic, the final time they sat at the table, with more pieces of paper being placed before him. Lorcan would not like how he parted with so much of their funds, but there was nothing to help it, given his situation.

"I love you," he said. "You know that, don't you?"

He didn't think she did. He watched Zoed laugh, realizing that, yes, maybe there could be death by volume, and this was a question he'd have to take some time mulling, on his own, along with several other questions, before joining up with Lorcan, who was hiding out at some fishing shack in southern Maine.

At night, on his wanderings, Dream Padraig passed by many Mollys. None of them said anything to him, as he walked, his pencil nub behind his ear, Walgreen's notebook in his pocket, in case inspiration struck. He made many trips to the assorted weapons shops, but he rarely bought anything, and when he did, he'd go to one of the bridges, over the Charles River, and take target practice at the smallmouth bass that swam below, their tail fins refracting bits of moonlight. The moon was always full during those nights.

He liked the walks enough though, and the peace they brought, that he began making a version of them during the day, when he was just Padraig, and Dream Padraig was off wherever he went to when he was not exploring about in the dark. He wrote Lorcan, care of a Maine game warden whom had once played a valuable role in their vintage Winchester rifle scam of a few years back, to inform his partner that he had sworn off the High Life, and the copious quantities of it that he was accustomed to enjoying.

"Nonetheless, my friend, it gave me an idea in mixology, so I am now blending ginger beer, which we drank so much of in days gone by, with the Islay whisky I've had no problem liberating from a local liquor store. I can get up to three bottles at time, if I stick one down my pants, though that is, I grant, a bit sophomoric. It's a nice fizzy blend. Stirs the imagination. And, as I have discovered, rouses Dream Padraig. He is making progress with Dream Molly. So, if it works out that actual Molly doesn't answer any of my letters, which I send her care of the dreadful Zoed, DP might have something worth living for with her. I think she's going to begin speaking soon. In this matter, the fizzy Scotch has proved invaluable."

Lorcan could not help but be worried about his friend. His letters spoke of restraint, balance, and maybe therapy. Long walks in the sunshine. And, above all, solidarity to their cause. And doing whatever was necessary to stay free.

But the more fizzy Scotch Padraig drank, the more he'd encounter Zoed, at night, at the various weapon stores, where he also must have had limitless credit. Zoed would laugh, and jab his finger, which would sometimes come loose from his hand, and intimate that the problems were just beginning for both Padraig and Dream Padraig, as he had lately come by new information, about their shared past.

"Is she after revenge for all of the volume?"

"She's got you over a barrel, fucker. State's evidence."

This was nettlesome. He began to have a harder time determining what was real, and what had been devised by others, to take him, as it were, down. Padraig crossed the whole of Boston and Cambridge every day, sweating, penning the occasional note for an eventual poem, trying to figure out if there was any overlap between what he saw and heard, in his brain, every night, as he slept, and what, really, was happening out in the world. It seemed too coincidental. If this was a movie, the one would have bearing on the other. And he had seen a lot of movies in a short time.

•

Lorcan was pleased when he finally had his friend back. They went crabbing every day in Maine, and ate the meat on rolls, while Lorcan drank cans of the High Life, and Padraig sipped his new whisky concoction.

"Bit tricky there for a bit, Lorc, bit tricky."

"Glad to be out of Boston?"

"Aye."

"Got the Dream Padraig bit sorted?"

"I think so. There were no weapon stores. That's how I could tell. Sometimes there were no weapon stores, but, I don't know, you felt dizzier when it wasn't real, and I was walking at a lively pace, and I hopped a few times, and even though it was very late, I was dead steadfast on my feet. But just to be sure, I went into one of those old cemeteries by the university, where the stones are practically piled one on top of each other. And I did a little race, like I was going around a maze. Still, dead steady."

"You went to his house?"

"No. I'd seen him a bunch on this bridge over the Charles. DP used to shoot smallmouth bass there. He'd smoke. A pipe. Most nights he was there. God knows I had followed him enough. No mucking about though. Given the precarious nature of the situation. So I just come up behind, right, let's do this, and man did that blade have to go through a lot of fat before I knew he was finished. He shat himself, actually. Then again, if he saw me coming, and knew what was going to happen to him, he probably would have shat himself more, so, in a sense, I did him a favor. With his dignity, and all. That's my one regret. And Molly, of course."

"Who's Molly?"

"Woman DP was making some headway with. And maybe a little more."

"A little more?"

"Or a little less. It's hard to tell sometimes. Fancy some more drinks and a quick nap?"

In the Chum

"So what you're saying is we're frozen right now?"

"Yes. Of course. Can you really not feel it?"

She tried to. But mostly she just watched. The waiters moved, no problem. She could see the water moving in her glass, like the table was buzzing. So maybe the table was moving. But she had always been the incredulous sort.

"And you knew that we'd be in this position?"

"You know I did. I kept telling you. Before you went away. For good. People go away in stages. As I have said."

She was tired of the theory-making. He made way too many theories. And predictions. They tended to go together. If such and such happens then such and such will be the end result. Like he was the hypothesis part of a lab report. But she was starting to feel it a little. She wanted a drink of the swirling water but her hands remained wherever they were. She couldn't see them. And she wasn't sure she could feel them.

"You can still feel things, after a fashion," he continued. "Touch. But that's not what I meant by frozen. It's like the bait."

Good God. Not the bait again. That quest of his. She heard the occasional report. After she left. How he scoured the town, and then the state, and then the entire region. He wrote her from his various outposts. He had a grease board. In a rucksack. And on it he'd tally up the words that were in each letter. He felt certain they were exact, although he never counted. He could simply tell.

Just like he could tell that someday they'd be frozen.

"I do feel colder now," she said, but he knew she wasn't understanding him, still.

"It's not like that." He tried to make his voice sound patient, and weary, which was not hard. All those years of upgrading his bait. From the tidal pools he got sea stars, razor clams, and small crabs who hadn't been bright enough to understand that the water would be rolling out again. Then he went to the pond. The walleye loved the razor clams, once you cracked them open. The rainbow trout were partial to the crabs, while the smaller blue gills, in particular, delighted in the arms of the sea stars.

But these were more than ordinary walleyes, trout, and blue gills. They were the best specimens anyone had ever found. He was certain of it. And, in actual fact, he was correct. With his bait, it took him only seconds until he had an entire rucksack full of fish, all of which would become bait unto themselves. He never questioned how they stayed alive in the rucksack. It was simply something they did. Maybe the grease board had something to do with it. Perhaps they enjoyed reading the numbers he entered on it, wondering about their significance, and if you had something to keep your mind occupied, whether you were man or beast, maybe that could stave off death. There were all kinds of reports out there. Had they ever had a child he figured he would have been strong enough, were that child pinned under a car, to lift up the vehicle, so that he could kick the baby out of harm's way. You'd be allowed to kick your child in such a scenario. Even she would see that. He had no doubt.

Just like he had no doubt that they'd be frozen. And that the walleyes, trout, and blue gills could be brought out to sea, where they'd haul in tuna, and sword fish, and tiger sharks, creatures who were so confounded by these fresh water delicacies that once they were in the boat he was able to club them over the head, without them knowing, really, what was going on. Like he had come upon them while they were reading.

He'd write her, about his adventures in baiting. How you take one discovery—for what was a caught fish like but a discovery—and build upon it, and build upon that, and on and on. He hoped the message would resonate with her. But instead, there was only silence. How many times had he wiped the grease board down, with the side of a fish that had felt bad for him, and his plight, and gave up his own life, in a display of fealty, such that he might prove useful as a grease board cleaner? Plenty of times, he lamented, one night, in the forest, as he sawed the heads off of his latest haul of tiger sharks, and placed them beneath white pines, like they were trail markers. And when the bears came to devour the tiger shark heads, he shot the bears, and sliced them up with a chainsaw, until they were in small enough portions that he could turn them into a stew, of sorts, in the industrial blender that he toted in a secondary rucksack. The bears made for excellent chum, and lampreys and hagfish and pale-colored lobsters, from the deepest deeps, made their way to the surface, all because of his chum. He wrote her of it. And his prodigious feats.

"It's more than chum," he said. "This is the stuff of my soul, of my new life's work, of my voyage of discovery. How can you not see how true I am? Why, there are lampreys and hagfish here. And you know how deep down they live. And now, they're at the surface. Am I content with them? Of course I'm not. That's why I turn every-thing into bait. Although you will doubt my motives. But eventually there will come a point where it all gets frozen. Locked in place. And it will be like all the words, duly marked on my grease board, and then wiped off again courtesy of the latest noble fish who, at least, empathizes with me, never existed."

He worried that they were like that all along. What did she read? Any of it? When he passed the million word mark, without receiving a single reply, he began to think that this was not merely a reflection of the fact that he lived in boats, in tree stands, in copses—and in caves, when he was lucky. The grease board could get a reprieve in the cave, so long as he had chalk, or a stone that could mimic chalk's effects. At first he sent the letters to the house. She'd have to go back, he figured. At some point. The house just sat there. And then the house was gone. Flat out gone. It was the first entity, between them, to go frozen. Naturally, when a house freezes over, it goes away completely. You can't just have a house that sits there, in-definitely, amongst other houses, with no trace of mo-tion. It atrophies. And once that occurs, it's only a matter of time. The house will go away, and so will the memo-ries that anyone had of it, such that when ersatz neigh-bors see the parcel of land on which his house once sat, they'll think, "someone really should build something on that vacant lot. It's an eyesore. Or we should turn it into a ball field or something. Probably too small for a ball field though."

He thought maybe the lot where his house had been would be handy as a place to dry his bait. Not all of his bait was alive. Some of it had to be dead. Plus, he could check and see if maybe she had left a message for him. Some sign on the ground that only he would understand, which could withstand the ravages of time and the weather, as his feelings for her had. He thought so, anyway. True, they had the good fortune of living inside his gut, and didn't have to get snowed on, or rained on, but there were juices in that gut, and they were probably more like acid rain than regular rain, so he thought it was quite the feat of love that those feelings remained. His letter on the subject was so lengthy that he marked half of its word count tally on his grease board, and the remaining portion on the ceiling of his latest cave. She knew, if she wanted to, where he was. He also printed the return address as clearly as possible.

After two million words, he really began to despair. He needed someone to talk to. Someone who would listen, mostly. Someone new. All the people who used to listen had become sick of doing so. They didn't tell him that, of course. But he knew. They thought, clearly: What else is there to say? Just as he knew, even more clearly, that there was always more to say, because these matters were infinitely nuanced, and if you were in such a matter, a new element of it would always occur to you. That's how time worked; it's what time did to you. He opened his rucksack, and stared at the face of one of his hagfish—his most trusted hagfish, in his mind—staring back at him.

"Consider, my friend, if you were hooked. You're on the line. I know we didn't meet that way. There was that chum, that good chum." He thought the hagfish made a subtle motion with his head, so he reached into a coffee can he had stuffed with bear chum and threw some of it on the creature's head. "So as I was saying: if you were hooked, on a line, and you were brought up to the surface, once you settled down and realized what was happening to you, you'd start to think, to make discoveries. They'd stop, probably when your journey to the air was over, if you weren't preserved properly, as I have preserved you. But let's say that you went along with the hook in your mouth for ages. The water didn't come to an end. After a few miles, people would get sick of hearing what you had to say. But you don't think new stuff would occur to you all the time, that you'd have new bits of information, fresh thoughts, worse epiphanies, after a million miles? Of course you would."

He wrote her that he felt so alone that he honestly considered bonding with the hagfish in that most delicate of ways. But even though he did not eat the hagfish, in his cave, the latter must have sensed something was up, because he was gone in the morning, leaving only a trail of mucus behind. While he was relieved that his friend had reacted in a clear-headed way, the sudden departure was a painful reminder. He wondered if this departure would splinter into levels of departure, like when she left. There's leaving, but that's just the start. Next was secondary leaving. First you have drowning, then you have secondary drowning, where some of the water that was hidden in some pocket of your lungs, or some nook inside of you—in following from the initial bout of drowning, which didn't quite kill you off—leaks out into a portion of your being where it can do some real harm. There was less water involved, the second time around, but it was deadlier water, because it came from the inside, and not the outside, and you hadn't a clue it was there, but boy were you ever going to. He shuddered, and spat repeatedly, and blew gobs of mucus out of his nose, lest the water was hidden away in his head, as he thought it may have been.

By the time he got to five million words—and who knows how many razor clams, small crabs, star fish, wall-eye, trout, blue gills, hagfish, lamprey, white lobsters, and bags of chum had passed through his rucksack—he could tell that they'd be frozen soon. It could have been that she no longer remembered that she had known him, or if his hair were brown, or if the color of his eyes matched, which they did not, which was strange, and would be all the more revealing of where he stood with someone if they forgot.

Once they were frozen there'd be nothing he could do about it. There'd be no words that could do anything at all, no passel of adventures in baiting and catching and re-baiting that could reanimate their lives together. She could want it as much as he wanted what he did as he paced in his caves, or tried to do so in his tree stands, sometimes forgetting where he was, and toppling over the sides, into a pile of leaves that he had assembled there, just in case. For that is how well he had come to know himself with the passing of all those words, and the latest haul, from the deep—the various deeps—of creatures.

He worried how it would feel to be frozen. Maybe it'd be alright. Your heart rate would slow down, so it'd be like being relaxed. He'd been relaxed before. After a few whiskies. Life slowed down. That was a great feeling. So much so that he resolved to try it during the day. He'd have to find an ideal rate of consumption, to keep him steady in gear, so to speak. Maybe one drink every other hour. She had disapproved. And so the angry years came to pass, when he overheated, during the day, but was so cool, so in control, at night, thanks to his carefully calibrated dosings. But she had gone to bed by then. For his overheated self had worn her out.

One of the lampreys had given him attitude. He tried to bite his hands with his funnel of a mouth, and its ring upon ring of downward slanting teeth. Granted, this lamprey ought to have been respected, in that he came from the deepest of depths, but that caused him to regard the lamprey as an enemy. He was scared of him. Not that he could admit that to himself. Normally, he'd examine, as closely as he could, each part of his latest haul. Sure, it was painful, and difficult to see the ravages those depths could make upon God's creatures. But this lamprey, he was a mess. He had scars and cuts in all sides of him. His jaw was flaking away at the top. His eyes were mismatched. Half of one was missing. His skin was yellowish. But he loved to bite all the same. He could control it. When offered a blade of grass, there was no biting then. But something warm and human and gentle—something defenseless, as his fingers had become, over those millions of words—and this lamprey almost came out of the rucksack to get his quarry. It was difficult to even look at him.

He felt guilty for the experiment, days before he resolved to undertake it. The guilt gave him headaches, like maybe not looking at the lamprey was praying on something he felt, sensed—though he tried not to—rather than articulated in himself, and punishing him with one migraine after another. Maybe. He didn't know. He wasn't sure he was in a place to know. That knowing might have made him into bait, only there wouldn't be someone around to make use of him as he had so adroitly made use of the creatures, or the parts of creatures, that had passed in and out of his rucksack.

He noted the shocked look on the lamprey's ravaged face as he took out a line with a huge hook on the end of it and threaded it through his back. The hole in the ice was waiting, along with a cinder block. He stuck the end of the line that had been in his hands under the cement block once he felt the lamprey hit the bottom. No one would eat him. Not this lamprey. He came from a place that other creatures didn't want anything to do with. He was certain. After three days—and more word tallies on the grease board in his rucksack, words that careened more than his words had previously—he returned to the hole and pulled up the frozen fish. Efforts were made to revive him, back in the cave, to see if, once frozen, one could become unfrozen. There was the briefest flicker of life, after a day or so. Nothing indicative of biting. It was obvious that the fish had something else on his mind. He was beckoning for an ear, so he leaned in close. There were no words, of course, but breathy little currents, which passed into his head, and gained translation in his mind. And with the processing of those words, the lamprey was hurled against the cave wall, and then smashed against it repeatedly, until he was a pulpy residue. The scene was sufficiently disturbing to send several hagfish on their way in the night, with trails of mucus to show for it.

With nothing better to do, he followed one of those trails. It took him past all the best grounds for finding bait, until he came to the patch of grass where he knew his house had once stood, before everyone forgot. Save for him. And maybe her. But it wouldn't matter anyway.

Something about the journey had dropped him into a different kind of lake, only he hadn't had the fortune, post-lake, of being mashed against a cave wall. For longer than he could tell, he watched the past harden. All of its component parts, which had been live, fleshy things, congealed, and then the rigor mortis set in, and there was no good any of those past words could do, no difference for them to make, even if she came across them in the future, and faced them like he could never face his guilt in those days leading up to the lamprey's final descent.

"Or, more to the point, his return to the surface. If you follow me."

She did. The waiters weren't moving so much after all. They were more like buoys, bobbing, than waiters, waiting.

"But I still…I love…I made…I think we can, after everything…"

The current would let them drift together for a bit. Currents were like that. She couldn't feel anything definite, anything particular, but rather this overwhelming totality. From all around.

"That'll be the ice," he shouted, as the distance widened. "Frozen."

He heard her thud against a buoy, and then again. She'd get used to it. It was difficult to get around the wind. He could write a book on the subject, he joked, as a lamprey, with mismatched eyes, and a scar in his back, swam up beside him.

"I don't suppose you're looking for a running buddy," he asked, but the creature just flashed his funnel of a mouth, with its rows and rows of downward slanted teeth.

"My God. How many rows have you got, sir? How many rows have you got?"

Lobby Lobsterson

Your keys, your keys, a kingdom for yours keys. Like they unlocked gates leading to worlds that a child's story book—not that you were ever going to have children— would deem enchanted. You always kept them in your right pants pocket, where they lived, often, with the coins you'd shove there after purchasing the morning's cup of coffee, and a phone that you programmed with the old- est ring tones you could find. When that synthesized lute sound would emanate from your pocket, the coins wouldn't jangle, for such was the paucity of volume, but neither would anything inside of you, until afterwards.

Isn't that always the way? Mothers have said so enough, and wheezy grandfathers who'd seen more of life than you had. You could paint a grandfather like nobody's business. Four or five came in over the past year. Paint my portrait, sir; we live in (an especially tony place) and I have heard good things about your work; I will not be around forever; we must leave our likenesses behind, for the next generation of—

Always a fancy name. A name that had what they used to call "good breeding." A name with Roman numerals after it, a skeleton key of its own that opened up a panorama of vast privilege, succession, modern peerage. They'd hack and they'd wheeze, and you'd wonder if you could paint a cough. Are you married, young man, they would ask, and you'd try to be nonchalant in directing their gaze with your brush, dangling it before you like the boney finger of the Ghost of Christmas Future in the direction of a small snapshot of a woman tacked to a wall where no one ever sat and posed. The remarks that followed did not vary much: what a beauty, look how kindness and clarity streams from her eyes, it's more than a likeness, something almost alive. It was a cheap photograph from a Walmart picture booth. Surely, your subject would add, you can't both live here, in this cramped space. No, no, you'd counter. We have a house as well. By the coast. This chuffed the old timers. Why, I have lived here my entire life, sir, as has eight generations of my family. And I can tell you, squarely, that we are by the coast; were you to open a window, we could smell the salt. My father's father's father's father's father's father made his fortune in ship building. By the coast indeed!

You were by the harbor, in a city, though. Quite different. Some day you would leave that city, when you had made a name for yourself, and become a country gentleman who was also an artist. Life would be more leisurely, more at your own pace, and you would be with her, far more often. That day, as you perceived it, was long in coming. So you screamed through the weekends when you were with her. You screamed through the car rides. You screamed to hear yourself scream, and you watched the rabble blow past you. The sons of people like the dynasty heads you'd paint, with their skeleton keys. How hard can you work, you'd ask. How far can I take this, how far can I push myself? Work is controllable. How much do you want it? How much can you bear? Don't just think you want it. Go out. And fucking want it. Line up at the far end of the field. What is the mind, after all, but a dark football pitch, over which a million balls bound. Sprint from one end of the pitch to the other and back, and back, and again, and vomit whatever is inside of you into the bucket at midfield. And then drink it back down, so you can vomit it again. And scream. She will understand.

Your keys, for your would-be kingdom, were on a decorative chain that you bought your second summer together, on a pier. Seven out of every ten shops sold ice cream at the coast, and closed with the first frost of the year. Or near about. Spring and ice cream made you feel hopeful. Maybe the larynx would get a rest, and the bees could go about their work, with their faces stuck down the bottom of the blooming flowers, without you rending the air and vibrating them needlessly, as she took the brunt of it. Pewter key chain. An embossed lobster climbing atop a trap. He's going to fall in, she said. But you don't know that. You can't know that. He could be taunting an enemy who had been foolish enough to get himself caught. Maybe he had a better understanding of how these things work. Maybe he had sold out. Maybe he worked for the man. Maybe he passed along his thoughts on the most efficacious designs. Maybe he was a screamer. You looked at her. You knew, of course, she wanted to say: Like you? She was too scared. Your mind would talk, but only to you, though the words, which you could never put together, were for her: you can level with me. You can call me what I am. Though I have given you no reason to believe that anything would be safe, after doing so. But I need it. And you need to do it. The joke is that I am not strong. The joke that you are not fully in on. The strength here is yours. These hard days and years, the volume, the if only's. The when will be's. The somedays are coming. The promise of being closer than one thinks. Then the key change. The musical key change, our song together in a better, more natural key. Down goes the volume. More of the coast, less of the harbor, four hands at the piano. The off-season ice cream shop, its windows shuttered, no longer a symbol for either of you, when you walked past it. And easeful bees, come the spring.

A kingdom for your keys, all the more so given that they cut. Too many of them on the ring, perhaps. Keys for cramped quarters by the harbor; keys for a house on the coast. The lobster made patterns in your flesh. His early efforts focused on breaking through the epidermis. Eventually, he managed it, and there were four pinprick marks. Then he began to saw. Patterns emerged. Different from the pattern of screams. The scions marched on. You did not. Come, she would say. Come away. What's going to happen is going to happen when it happens. Seascapes flashed by the windows as the you rode with her, slumped down in the passenger seat, on your way to the coast. Material for a million ham-and-eggers who had ever brought brush to canvas. Some of whom had surely marched on and past you. Please. Trust me. Please. It is going to happen. You don't need to go on like this. Your time is just a different time, but it is coming. Sometimes you would then make a vulgar joke that was not supposed to be funny.

Fie on top of fie. Right. What would she know, anyway, what could she know. The pain in that car. When do you first become aware that someone else's is greater than your own, and that it stems from your own, and is a result of feeling inconsolable not about what that individual is going through, but what you are going through? Does it always have to be after? Did the grandfathers who knew better than you did have an answer? Did the mothers? Would they have been grandfathers or mothers if they knew the answer? Did they have cold, clinical engravers in their pocket as you did? Probably not. You began to think he was trying to tell you something, especially on Sundays. There was intercourse on Sundays. Always Sundays, and then back to the harbor, come Sunday night. Bounce, from one to another. From hole to hole. And there was that, too, and it was with love, the embrace of love, always real, always affirming, never leaden, never the stuff of screams, despite the newly forming memories of the latest din.

What can you see in these situations? What can you be made to see? The jokes amongst the rage, the rare, random, fleeting moment when the humor cuts through, but retains a certain grimness, a portentousness, all the same. Christmas at the coast. You pick the movie, dear. Oh, no, not *A Christmas Carol* again. Okay. Smile, laugh, indulgence, but happy indulgence. She starts to hope: Maybe he will remain here, with me, as a part of us. Less shuttling, back and forth. Maybe the old men, with their commendable breeding, can come here. The sea air—something to do them good. His name will be bigger. He's closer than he thinks he is. I can ride this out with him. We wait for the click, the turn, the lining up of tumblers. The lock has been sprung. I know him. Who he is, really. Who he is under better circumstances, the circumstances he deserves. No matter what other people say. My parents. The closeness when he is inside of me. That has never been corrupted. Reaching my fingers up myself last night after he had gone, again, on that train. The stickiness and the smoothness of it, the taste upon my lips, the vague hint of salt, and something still warm between us. You can do this. You can hold out. But—maybe. It's later now. I still believe. I have no doubt. But am I safe? Am I emotionally safe? The volume. My right ear. I know I am hearing better out of the left one. The things he says to me; who could believe them, who could believe they come from someone who, I believe, loves me? Would he be better off on his own? I don't think he screams when he is by himself. It is later still. Where have I gone? What has swallowed me up? Have I disappeared, like paint, into some kind of canvas? Hello? Please? Anyone? Me? Who is me, what is me, where is me, why me. From whence, from where, from why. He is crueler now. Always crueler. We wait for the tumblers of the lock. I know they will click, he does not. I still know it. Despite everything I no longer know. I can't reach him. I can't reach me. His leg was all cut up tonight. His right thigh. He said his key chain did it. Those patterns. Like miniature horseshoe prints. A faint, scabby branding. When I brought my hand to it, there was something there. While he was taking his shirt off. I know it must not be very painful, but it felt painful to me. I saw how he looked at me in that moment. He believed me then. No screaming. No allegations. He saw that I cared. Maybe. Maybe that will (blank); maybe it will lead to (blank); maybe it will bring on this, bring on that; maybe it's a start of something, the end of something else. He hates maybes.

Don't make a joke about how if you were Ebenezer Scrooge, you would come through the experience untransformed. Maybe that is a go-to joke. Jokes made with regularity, the thinking goes, become jokier, losing any resonance as actual, factual commentary. The empty house. Everything, every last tea cup, gone. There are various forms of departure, in these matters. One may get off the train, and end one's walk to one's house and see that one or two items are amiss. A pair of shoes that is always in the same place upon your return, has now up and set off on an adventure, probably outside of the house. The trip to the bathroom follows. Ah, Mr. Toothbrush is off on an adventure as well; he has probably absconded with the shoes. And you thought they wouldn't get along. Maybe there is a note; is there a need? Not necessarily. But information can be useful, because you will think, no matter what, that you are lacking some. In other instances, one's keys are rendered impotent, or, at least, incapable of bringing everything off, properly, once they enter into the front door lock. In, and all the way in, but incapable of moving left, or right. Blue balls for keys. Or else, it's like that first day. The realtor threw open the door, and there it was: the house for when the maybe's stopped with their half-measures, and became really's and definitely's and without-a-doubt's. The click of the tumblers. Accordance. You, sir, have come from wherever you were, to get where you thought you needed to be. And now, you can be: you, her. There's you done, and there's you started. She waited it out, didn't she?

But the lobster knew better all along, and he kept cutting. And there it was at the top of your right thigh on that day, a wound that you could not see, but felt through your pants, that seemed to throb and deepen, enough so that were anyone to doubt its legitimacy, you could direct them to raise a finger and stick it in as far as it would go. They wouldn't have so much as touched the sides. Every last fork, gone. Door mats. Total, definitive, highly efficient. Every last fork seems to hurt more than the one big couch. Who knew? A tumbleweed would not have been out of place, if a greater length of time had passed, and this tumbleweed possessed a more efficient key of its own. A key that got its release. You go to wherever you are going to go. You phone, you write, you text, you barter with God, you think about the nightmares you've had from which you could not awake as you prayed that they were nightmares, and you suddenly feel more corporal, as if to say, this is anything but a nightmare, boyo. Crack yourself in the head if you like. You will find no sheets, pillows, or pools of drool here. You're on your own.

Just about. The lobster gives a tap. Hello. I guess it is just you and I. And you think, come on now, this is hard enough. I am realizing things. Oh my good God, for fuck's sake. For fuck's sake, what have I done, what was I doing. Will anyone believe me now? Could anyone believe what I am claiming to know now, after so much—everything? Could she? Is that possible? Could I, were I her? You walk past a church you never go into. You don't care about the church, save that it's supposed to be historic. People who are long ago dead and well known, people whom you'd like to be counted amongst some day, have been there. That is your interest, up until this particular afternoon, and you and the lobster, and the quarry he jeers at inside the trap he is perched upon, go through those church doors. You kneel there, feeling like a twat, an interloper, so you stand, and walk over to the terraced rows and rows of guttering candles beneath a stained glass window depicting someone and some story that you surmise probably means a great deal to some people, given its proximity to the candles, which seem important. You have a five dollar bill because you gave her one with a tear in it. She was genial, and people took to her; the cashier wouldn't give her the gruff he'd give you with damaged currency, and she was, of course, thoughtful enough to replace it. Should you part with it, you think, as you rub it through your fingers, knowing she had touched it, and recently, and maybe this was as close as you'd ever get again. As atoms touching atoms. But into the slot it goes; maybe something karmic will transpire in the lighting of two candles with her five dollar note. Six old women call the rosary. Their vigor suggests they do so every day. You have never painted any of them, and, from the look of their clothes, their husbands either.

Three days later. Might as well be 130 days later, or 330 days. You calculate in your head: if three days feels like 130, roughly, what will 130 feel like? Will I make it there? The five dollar note has not paid off, as you wanted it to. Had you retained it, you could do the atom to atom thing, at least. What's left for that? The lobster saws away, so you take down your pants to see how his work is progressing. He is consistent. You admire him for that. He works the same pattern over and over again. Can you bond with him? Maybe address him with a snappy nickname? You try Lobby Lobsterson. He ignores you, and continues to saw and abrade, a diligent worker. You wonder if he can ply his trade anywhere else, or if he can only work your wounds. You pull an ancient fruitcake out of the refrigerator that has sat there since Christmas, and you sit him on top of it, and leave him for a day. Nothing. You purchase some turkey from the deli; maybe he needs to work upon softer stuff. Another day, nothing. Back in the pocket he goes, and, as soon as he hits bottom, he returns to work. Rip and saw, rip and saw, scrape, chafe, dig, stab. Sharpen up the contours of the pattern. You grow tired of the dull ache, and your inability to bond, despite letting Lobby indulge himself, and you grow resentful. So out he comes. You only need two of the keys now anyway, so you buy a cheap tin ring from the hardware store, and the cutting stops. Until you realize that her fingers had been there, and with the five dollar note being gone, this is all you have, atom to atom-wise. So first you try your fingernails, which you've let grow long for this purpose, after Lobby's work begins to heal over. You don't want to give him the satisfaction of being the only sculpture in the place, not with his frustrating attitude, but you wonder if it would be wise to ask him for tips, not that he would likely give you any. Fuck him, you think, and hurl him as hard as you can into the far corner of the room, where he chips the paint and falls to the ground. The fingernails don't cut it, but you have a knife in the kitchen drawer, and that works well. Every night you cut away, and you maintain the pattern, and you touch it, and you bring your fingers to your mouth sometimes, like she told you she would, on occasion, after you had left, and she could feel your seed moving about inside of her. Salty, you think. And you cut, and you cut, and you cut, believing you had purity of purpose, at least in this, and there was nothing else you could do, so far as the two of you went. You would not paint the pattern, because it was impossible to do so, regardless of the talent you possessed or believed you did. It was elsewhere, and it was something else, not scab, blood, and horseshoe shapes designed by a lobster who would not speak to you.

I Want to Dance Where the Children Play

He stood outside the fitness center and watched the women work out in gym suits and leotards that reminded him of sitcoms from the Seventies. There were many fitness centers in the city where he sometimes worked, but this was the one he stopped at. He watched the men, too. Most of them tried not to watch the women. Some watched the women directly, though. There was a message painted on the far wall across from where he preferred to stand while he watched the men and the women. "This is a no judgement zone." That suited him, even if no one had thought to check the spelling. The glass was always very clean, despite being at ground level, where sandwich wrappers and coffee cups whipped around and sometimes bounced off the glass. The wind could be overpowering. The workout center and the tall building across the way made a wind tunnel. Men stood on beams and went up and down the side of the tall building with ropes and pulleys, cleaning the glass. They did not look down at the fitness center. He tried to be respectful of people and their boundaries, so he bought some chalk and drew a line five feet in front of the glass so he had a spot where he could stand courteously and watch the men and women and read the sign on the far wall. One time he thought he had seen a man meet a woman for the first time and that they would not be apart again. That made him feel warm when it was very cold out and the wind blew through the tunnel and he couldn't see his chalk line beneath the snow.

•

Once, he stood in the easement beside his house and watched men load a truck they had parked in the woods. The woods provided good cover. He admired preparation. There was a dirt road that led to a paved road. A long time ago it had been used to walk cows, two-by-two, down to a pasture that had been paved over. There were basketball courts atop the pasture now. Sometimes he watched the boys who used to play there and he kept score in his head. He would also officiate, in a whisper. "That was a travel." "That was a double dribble. "That was a three second violation." He believed he knew the boys well enough to be able to tell when one or the other would try to get away with something. Naturally, he did not want to encroach upon their game, but he didn't need any chalk to stop him from that. There were rock walls fifteen yards away from the court, on the north and south side, and he would stand behind one of them. They marked property lines long before he had been there. Long before there were basketballs. One boy would dance when he made a basket from behind the giant semicircle that extended far from the basket. The younger boy did not care for the dance, but sometimes he would see him start to smile. "This would be a good place for a sign like the one at my fitness center," he thought whenever he passed and the boys were not there. But signs could not be written on the air. He did not know how to hang one either. Maybe he could erect some poles and get some twine and a canvas. He wasn't sure which spelling to use either: whether it was more important to be grammatically precise, or if that was not in the spirit of the original piece. He reached in his pocket for another piece of chalk, and found himself squeezing a pebble as he thought of the older boy and the dance he liked to make behind the giant semicircle.

•

He stood and watched the items leave the house. A cardinal on a low maple bough watched with him. He hoped that the cardinal would not blow his cover. He'd read about situations like these. There was no sense in trying to be a hero. The cardinal was very quiet, at least. He remembered that the cardinal was a star, of sorts, among his fellows. He was the state bird for seven states. That was the record. He decided to call this one Seven. He was an especially attentive cardinal. They both watched the two men carry out the items that were now theirs. Decorative plates with gold inlay and borders; a computer; several televisions; a set of knives; an exercise machine that he had grown tired of; a collection of old baseball statues from when he was a boy; a video game console; more exercise machines. His wife would not be pleased to learn about that. The men never ran. They walked briskly. He wondered what they would do if it were raining and if that would make a difference. He couldn't remember if it was better to walk or run when it began to rain. Someone once told him that running would only make you get wetter. He wasn't so sure about that. One day, he determined, he would conduct some experiments. The cardinal remained on his bough, unblinking. He didn't know whether cardinals could blink anyway, or whether it'd be best to walk or fly in the rain, if he were a bird. It would probably depend on whether or not he really needed to be some place, and how quickly, he decided. He thought about maybe conducting some avian-based experiments in the future, as well, but that probably would have been much trickier.

•

He stood and listened to everyone tell him how wonderful his work was. "It is so lifelike. How do you do it?" "This is art of the highest order. And in the least likely of mediums." People were often complimenting themselves, he thought, when they tried to compliment others in a fancy way. Sometimes, while they talked, he worried that he would not make it to the gym in time to watch the men and women, and maybe see a scene like that time he watched one man meet one woman whom it seemed he would then know forever. There would be other days, at least. "You, sir, have true artistic moxie. Could you do something for my son's bar mitzvah? Of course, you'd have to clear the subject material with my wife. Or maybe you could provide a horse for Sophie's Sweet Sixteen party? You know how she loves her dressage." He did not. The cardinal had begun to shrink. The basketball was becoming rectangular. The life-size running woman was losing her hair. It drained into her neck. That was always the way. He wasn't sure if it had been wise to arrange the two boys such that they were holding hands. Maybe they weren't far enough away in age for that kind of thing. Society changes so rapidly, he thought. But that was not a problem now. The younger boy's hand was a puddle on the ground. It was time for the disco ball. The parents of the children of whatever youth sports association had hired him were about to dance. He looked at his watch, and then at his work. There was still a long way to go. He would not be able to make it to the fitness center before it closed, and it would, of course, be too dark where the pasture had once been. The dancers began to crowd closer. He reached into his pocket for his chalk and got down on his knees to make a semicircle around his work. He stepped inside the semicircle like the younger boy did at the basketball court. A drunken woman danced up to him. "Hey, Ice Man! What are you doing just standing there! Why don't you come and have a dance? Why else are you hanging around here?" He looked at his chalk line, and then his watch, and then his work. "I need to see them melt." The eyes of the cardinal streamed down his beak. He thought about trying to drink some of him, and got on his knees to do so. The janitor's mop hit him on his right thigh. "Job's hard enough, man." He hugged the janitor and raced off to the fitness center. He knew it would be closed, but he could freshen up his chalk line for tomorrow, in the moonlight.

Catalogue Nocturne

The first performance: me sitting in a car. There was no one around. It was gray, threatening rain. The car wouldn't start. It was at the end of a road—a country road—that led into a busier one. One that was normally busy. I was facing the direction of our house, the one I shared with my parents, in that childhood I told you about. You were behind me, back the other way, in a very woodsy part of the town. On a street with a kid I was friends with; a pretty bad guy, actually. You weren't with him. Just on his street, a few houses down. I don't know how I know, but that's how these things work, don't they? The town is one winding road after another, with lots of inclines. Very woodsy. So, it can take fifteen or twenty minutes to get from a place like my family's house, to this kid's house. I was facing the wrong direction anyway though, and the car wouldn't start. No one was out, as I have said, everything was gray, except these signs that hung on poles high above everything. They were adverts for that farm we use to go to, when we had a house of our own. And no, it didn't matter that it was 500 miles away. A loyal clientele is a good clientele.

And then we were on a train. We were where we are now. It was all the same. Somehow, we ended up on the same line. We could not talk. I tried to talk. You cried. It was an old train—the kind that Holmes and Watson rode on. There was to be an awards ceremony. A fat man won some award and there was a procession, with him going from one end of the train to the other, despite how cramped everything was. I was at the front of it. He wound up and gave me a huge handshake, very vigorous. Our hands didn't correctly look into place though, and it was an awkward grip. I knew how far back you were, and after he passed me, I knew when he'd reach where you were. We got off together, you and me. We were both going to that town where our own house had been. Different matters of business. You had a cooking class. It was gray again. No rain, but it looked like it was coming. We got off in a field, not in our town, our former town, but not far. We both knew as much. The center portion was paved. There was a bench. We ended up on it. We kissed. It was not anticipated. There was a bus by the bench. Kids were on a field trip. We had not seen it before. It was over our heads now, almost, at a strange angle. The kids laughed. We ended up back on the train. The fat man had cleared out. I thought I saw some streamers under a seat. We got off again, certain that neither of us would see the other, but there were, once more. What are the chances? But a person has to eat, and so we came to the same cafeteria. It was for adults only. There were not many of them. It was a very spacious cafeteria. I tried to get you to talk to me, after what had happened in the field. You started to, and then tried to stop yourself. The words came out though, and so you began stuffing wadded up pieces of napkin in your mouth, to check their flow. I pulled them out, to hear you, and you put in more, and started to choke. I got the last of them out, at least, and you ran to the door, and out into the field, crying.

The sound of the hydraulic lift. The evening's concluding

piece. We were in your car, pulling into a garage. Not the garage in that town, not too far from our town, our former town, that we broke down in. A man on my side took my order for coffee. I ordered a large iced, just milk. We were going to stay in the car throughout the inspection of its underside. This was very important, for some reason. It is why they had the coffee service, as I understood it. I discovered that you were in the backseat, behind me. You were trying to get out. I offered you some coffee. You said your dad sold it to me. He worked here, that was his job. How could I not know. You were crying. Starting to, anyway. I apologized. You were in the front seat now. You told me you were wet; as you told me, you were grinding against my hand. I felt you climax on it. Your tears had gotten into your hair, and your sweat, and I pressed my head into your hair. Your hair is not the comforter, but I know there is some of it under the bed.

Colin Fleming

Colin Fleming writes for *The Atlantic, The New Yorker, Rolling Stone, Slate, Vanity Fair, The New York Times Book Review, ESPN The Magazine, The Washington Post, The New Criterion*, and *JazzTimes*. His fiction appears in *The Iowa Review, Boulevard, Black Clock, Michigan Quarterly Review, TriQuarterly, PEN America, Denver Quarterly, Slice, Green Mountains Review*, and *The Massachusetts Review*. He is the author of *Between Cloud and Horizon: A Relationship Casebook in Stories* (Texas Review Press, 2013). Find him on the web at colinfleminglit.com.

Jenny Gorecki

Jenny Gorecki has a BFA in Studio Arts from the University of Illinois at Chicago and a certificate from the Virginia Commonwealth University Sculpture program. She also studied painting in Rome, Italy. Her website is jennygorecki.com.

CPSIA information can be obtained at www.ICGtesting.com
Printed in the USA
LVOW07s2338220216

476268LV00006B/359/P